DOVER · THRIFT · EDITIONS

The Double

FYODOR DOSTOYEVSKY

DOVER PUBLICATIONS, INC.
Mineola, New York

DOVER THRIFT EDITIONS

GENERAL EDITOR: STANLEY APPELBAUM
EDITOR OF THIS VOLUME: ADAM FROST

Copyright

Published in Canada by General Publishing Company, Ltd., 30 Lesmill Road, Don Mills, Toronto, Ontario.
Published in the United Kingdom by Constable and Company, Ltd., 3 The Lanchesters, 162–164 Fulham Palace Road, London W6 9ER.

Bibliographical Note

This Dover edition, first published in 1997, contains the unabridged text of *The Double,* translated by Constance Garnett, as published in *Fyodor Dostoevsky: The Eternal Husband and Other Stories* by William Heinemann, Ltd., London, 1917. The Note was prepared specially for this edition.

Library of Congress Cataloging-in-Publication Data

Dostoyevsky, Fyodor, 1821–1881.
    [Dvoĭnik. English]
    The Double / Fyodor Dostoyevsky.
        p.   cm. — (Dover thrift editions)
    ISBN 0-486-29572-9 (pbk.)
    I. Title.   II. Series.
PG3326.D8   1997
891.73'3—dc20   96-38924
                                                                              CIP

Manufactured in the United States of America
Dover Publications, Inc., 31 East 2nd Street, Mineola, N.Y. 11501

Note

FYODOR DOSTOYEVSKY (1821–1881) was born and raised in Moscow, where he was educated before attending the School of Military Engineers in St. Petersburg. After three years in the army, Dostoyevsky resigned to devote himself to writing, and in 1845 his first novel, *Poor Folk*, appeared. It was published to great acclaim, its author hailed as a powerful new voice in Russian literature.

In *The Double: A Petersburg Poem* (1846), his second novel, Dostoyevsky introduced a theme to which he would return throughout his career: that of the self divided. After a series of misfortunes has put him in a precarious emotional state, the clerk Golyadkin seems to encounter a man who is not only his spitting image, but who shares his name and background as well. This doppelgänger is successful in business and in his dealings with his fellow man—in everything, that is, in which the real Golyadkin is not—and his presence ultimately leads his counterpart to the brink of madness. Golyadkin's dual nature is echoed in Dostoyevsky's later works, reflected in the many characters torn apart by moral or emotional conflicts.

The years following the publication of *The Double* found Dostoyevsky increasingly involved in politics. In 1849 he was arrested, tried and sentenced to death for treasonous activities: at the last moment, when Dostoyevsky was only seconds away from execution, the sentence was commuted to eight years of hard labor in Siberia. His time in the penal colony did much to shape the author's political and religious beliefs, bringing him away from his youthful liberal leanings and toward the orthodoxy of the Russian church; it did much as well to exacerbate the epilepsy that would haunt him for the rest of his life. After serving four years of his sentence, Dostoyevsky was released and conscripted into the army. He did not return to St. Petersburg until 1859.

Dostoyevsky wrote his most widely recognized novels during the last seventeen years of his life, when he had already been writing for twenty years. *Notes from the Underground* (1864) was the first of these novels, followed by *Crime and Punishment* (1866), *The Idiot* (1868–69), *The Demons* (1871) and *The Brothers Karamazov* (1880): the planned sequel to this last book was left unrealized when the author died suddenly on 9 February 1881, of causes stemming from his epilepsy. By the time of his death, Dostoyevsky had become widely recognized for his ability to dramatize the many social, intellectual and moral problems that confront mankind. His reputation has since extended far beyond his native country, and his books have influenced the works of such authors as Nietzsche, Malraux and Sartre.

Contents

CHAPTER I

IT was a little before eight o'clock in the morning when Yakov Petro-vitch Golyadkin, a titular councillor, woke up from a long sleep. He yawned, stretched, and at last opened his eyes completely. For two min-utes, however, he lay in his bed without moving, as though he were not yet quite certain whether he were awake or still asleep, whether all that was going on around him were real and actual, or the continuation of his confused dreams. Very soon, however, Mr. Golyadkin's senses began more clearly and more distinctly to receive their habitual and everyday impressions. The dirty green, smoke-begrimed, dusty walls of his little room, with the mahogany chest of drawers and chairs, the table paint-ed red, the sofa covered with American leather of a reddish colour with little green flowers on it, and the clothes taken off in haste overnight and flung in a crumpled heap on the sofa, looked at him familiarly. At last the damp autumn day, muggy and dirty, peeped into the room through the dingy window pane with such a hostile, sour grimace that Mr. Golyadkin could not possibly doubt that he was not in the land of Nod, but in the city of Petersburg, in his own flat on the fourth storey of a huge block of buildings in Shestilavotchny Street. When he had made this important discovery Mr. Golyadkin nervously closed his eyes, as though regretting his dream and wanting to go back to it for a moment. But a minute later he leapt out of bed at one bound, probably all at once grasping the idea about which his scattered and wandering thoughts had been revolving. From his bed he ran straight to a little round looking-glass that stood on his chest of drawers. Though the sleepy, short-sighted countenance and rather bald head reflected in the looking-glass were of such an insignificant type that at first sight they would certainly not have attracted particular attention in any one, yet the owner of the countenance was satisfied with all that he saw in the looking-glass. "What a thing it would be," said Mr. Golyadkin in an

1

undertone, "what a thing it would be if I were not up to the mark to-day, if something were amiss, if some intrusive pimple had made its appearance, or anything else unpleasant had happened; so far, however, there's nothing wrong, so far everything's all right."

Greatly relieved that everything was all right, Mr. Golyadkin put the looking-glass back in its place and, although he had nothing on his feet and was still in the attire in which he was accustomed to go to bed, he ran to the little window and with great interest began looking for something in the courtyard, upon which the windows of his flat looked out. Apparently what he was looking for in the yard quite satisfied him too; his face beamed with a self-satisfied smile. Then, after first peeping, however, behind the partition into his valet Petrushka's little room and making sure that Petrushka was not there, he went on tiptoe to the table, opened the drawer in it and, fumbling in the furthest corner of it, he took from under old yellow papers and all sorts of rubbish a shabby green pocket-book, opened it cautiously, and with care and relish peeped into the furthest and most hidden fold of it. Probably the roll of green, grey, blue, red and particoloured notes looked at Golyadkin, too, with approval: with a radiant face he laid the open pocketbook before him and rubbed his hands vigorously in token of the greatest satisfaction. Finally, he took it out—his comforting roll of notes—and, for the hundredth time since the previous day, counted them over, carefully smoothing out every note between his forefinger and his thumb.

"Seven hundred and fifty roubles in notes," he concluded at last, in a half-whisper. "Seven hundred and fifty roubles, a noteworthy sum! It's an agreeable sum," he went on, in a voice weak and trembling with gratification, as he pinched the roll with his fingers and smiled significantly; "it's a very agreeable sum! A sum agreeable to any one! I should like to see the man to whom that would be a trivial sum! There's no knowing what a man might not do with a sum like that. . . . What's the meaning of it, though?" thought Mr. Golyadkin; "where's Petrushka?" And still in the same attire he peeped behind the partition again. Again there was no sign of Petrushka; and the samovar standing on the floor was beside itself, fuming and raging in solitude, threatening every minute to boil over, hissing and lisping in its mysterious language, to Mr. Golyadkin something like, "Take me, good people, I'm boiling and perfectly ready."

"Damn the fellow," thought Mr. Golyadkin. "That lazy brute might really drive a man out of all patience; where's he dawdling now?"

In just indignation he went out into the hall, which consisted of a little corridor at the end of which was a door into the entry, and saw his servant surrounded by a good-sized group of lackeys of all sorts, a mixed rabble from outside as well as from the flats of the house. Petrushka was telling something, the others were listening. Apparently the subject of the conversation, or the conversation itself, did not please Mr. Golyadkin. He promptly called Petrushka and returned to his room, displeased and even upset. "That beast would sell a man for a halfpenny, and his master before any one," he thought to himself: "and he has sold me, he certainly has. I bet he has sold me for a farthing. Well?"

"They've brought the livery, sir."

"Put it on, and come here."

When he had put on his livery, Petrushka, with a stupid smile on his face, went in to his master. His costume was incredibly strange. He had on a much-worn green livery, with frayed gold braid on it, apparently made for a man a yard taller than Petrushka. In his hand he had a hat trimmed with the same gold braid and with a feather in it, and at his hip hung a footman's sword in a leather sheath. Finally, to complete the picture, Petrushka, who always liked to be in *negligé*, was barefooted. Mr. Golyadkin looked at Petrushka from all sides and was apparently satisfied. The livery had evidently been hired for some solemn occasion. It might be observed, too, that during his master's inspection Petrushka watched him with strange expectancy and with marked curiosity followed every movement he made, which extremely embarrassed Mr. Golyadkin.

"Well, and how about the carriage?"

"The carriage is here too."

"For the whole day?"

"For the whole day. Twenty-five roubles."

"And have the boots been sent?"

"Yes."

"Dolt! can't even say, 'Yes, sir.' Bring them here."

Expressing his satisfaction that the boots fitted, Mr. Golyadkin asked for his tea, and for water to wash and shave. He shaved with great care and washed as scrupulously, hurriedly sipped his tea and proceeded to the principal final process of attiring himself: he put on an almost new pair of trousers; then a shirtfront with brass studs, and a very bright and agreeably flowered waistcoat; about his neck he tied a gay, particoloured cravat, and finally drew on his coat, which was also newish and carefully brushed. As he dressed, he more than once looked lovingly at his boots, lifted up first one leg and then the other, admired their shape, kept muttering something to himself, and from time to time made expressive grimaces. Mr. Golyadkin was, however, extremely absent-minded that morning, for he scarcely noticed the little smiles and grimaces made at his expense by Petrushka, who was helping him dress. At last, having arranged everything properly and having finished dressing, Mr. Golyadkin put his pocketbook in his pocket, took a final admiring look at Petrushka, who had put on his boots and was therefore also quite ready, and, noticing that everything was done and that there was nothing left to wait for, he ran hurriedly and fussily out on to the stairs, with a slight throbbing at his heart. The light-blue hired carriage with a crest on it rolled noisily up to the steps. Petrushka, winking to the driver and some of the gaping crowd, helped his master into the carriage; and, hardly able to suppress an idiotic laugh, shouted in an unnatural voice: "Off!" jumped up on the footboard, and the whole turnout, clattering and rumbling noisily, rolled into the Nevsky Prospect. As soon as the light-blue carriage dashed out of the gate, Mr. Golyadkin rubbed his hands convulsively and went off into a slow, noiseless chuckle, like a jubilant man who has succeeded in bringing off a splendid performance and is as pleased as Punch with the performance himself. Immediately after his access of gaiety, however, laughter was replaced by a strange and anxious expression on the face of Mr. Golyadkin. Though the weather was damp and muggy, he let down both windows of the carriage and began carefully scrutinizing the passers-by to left and to right, at once assuming a decorous and sedate air when he thought any one was looking at him. At the turning from Liteyny Street into the Nevsky Prospect he was startled by a most unpleasant sensation and, frowning like some poor wretch whose corn has been accidentally trodden on, he huddled with almost panic-stricken haste into the darkest corner of his carriage.

He had seen two of his colleagues, two young clerks serving in the same government department. The young clerks were also, it seemed to Mr. Golyadkin, extremely amazed at meeting their colleague in such a way; one of them, in fact, pointed him out to the other. Mr. Golyadkin even fancied that the other had actually called his name, which, of course, was very unseemly in the street. Our hero concealed himself and did not respond. "The silly youngsters!" he began reflecting to himself. "Why, what is there strange in it? A man in a carriage, a man needs to be in a carriage, and so he hires a carriage. They're simply noodles! I know them—simply silly youngsters, who still need thrashing! They want to be paid a salary for playing pitch-farthing and dawdling about, that's all they're fit for. I'd let them all know, if only . . ."

Mr. Golyadkin broke off suddenly, petrified. A smart pair of Kazan horses, very familiar to Mr. Golyadkin, in a fashionable droshky, drove rapidly by on the right side of his carriage. The gentleman sitting in the droshky, happening to catch a glimpse of Mr. Golyadkin, who was rather incautiously poking his head out of the carriage window, also appeared to be extremely astonished at the unexpected meeting and, bending out as far as he could, looked with the greatest curiosity and interest into the corner of the carriage in which our hero made haste to conceal himself. The gentleman in the droshky was Andrey Filippovitch, the head of the office in which Mr. Golyadkin served in the capacity of assistant to the chief clerk. Mr. Golyadkin, seeing that Andrey Filippovitch recognized him, that he was looking at him open-eyed and that it was impossible to hide, blushed up to his ears.

"Bow or not? Call back or not? Recognize him or not?" our hero wondered in indescribable anguish, "or pretend that I am not myself, but somebody else strikingly like me, and look as though nothing were the matter. Simply not I, not I—and that's all," said Mr. Golyadkin, taking off his hat to Andrey Filippovitch and keeping his eyes fixed upon him. "I'm . . . I'm all right," he whispered with an effort; "I'm . . . quite all right. It's not I, it's not I—and that is the fact of the matter."

Soon, however, the droshky passed the carriage, and the magnetism of his chief's eyes was at an end. Yet he went on blushing, smiling and muttering something to himself. . .

"I was a fool not to call back," he thought at last. 'I ought to have taken a bolder line and behaved with gentlemanly openness. I ought to have said 'This is how it is, Andrey Filippovitch, I'm asked to the dinner too,' and that's all it is!"

Then, suddenly recalling how taken aback he had been, our hero flushed as hot as fire, frowned, and cast a terrible defiant glance at the front corner of the carriage, a glance calculated to reduce all his foes to ashes. At last, he was suddenly inspired to pull the cord attached to the driver's elbow, and stopped the carriage, telling him to drive back to Liteyny Street. The fact was, it was urgently necessary for Mr. Golyadkin, probably for the sake of his own peace of mind, to say something very interesting to his doctor, Krestyan Ivanovitch. And, though he had made Krestyan Ivanovitch's acquaintance quite recently, having, indeed, only paid him a single visit, and that one the previous week, to consult him about some symptom. But a doctor, as they say, is like a priest, and it would be stupid for him to keep out of sight, and, indeed, it was his duty to know his patients. "Will it be all right, though," our hero went on, getting out of the carriage at the door of a five-storey house in Liteyny Street, at which he had told the driver to stop the carriage: "Will it be all right? Will it be proper? Will it be appropriate?

After all, though," he went on, thinking as he mounted the stairs out of breath and trying to suppress the beating of his heart, which had the habit of beating on all other people's staircases: "After all, it's on my own business and there's nothing reprehensible in it. . . . It would be stupid to keep out of sight. Why, of course, I shall behave as though I were quite all right, and have simply looked in as I passed. . . . He will see, that it's all just as it should be."

Reasoning like this, Mr. Golyadkin mounted to the second storey and stopped before flat number five, on which there was a handsome brass door-plate with the inscription—

KRESTYAN IVANOVITCH RUTENSPITZ
Doctor of Medicine and Surgery

Stopping at the door, our hero made haste to assume an air of propriety, ease, and even of a certain affability, and prepared to pull the bell. As he was about to do so he promptly and rather appropriately reflected that it might be better to come to-morrow, and that it was not very pressing for the moment. But as he suddenly heard footsteps on the stairs, he immediately changed his mind again and at once rang Krestyan Ivanovitch's bell—with an air, moreover, of great determination.

CHAPTER II

THE doctor of medicine and surgery, Krestyan Ivanovitch Rutenspitz, a very hale, though elderly man, with thick eyebrows and whiskers that were beginning to turn grey, eyes with an expressive gleam in them that looked capable of routing every disease, and, lastly, with orders of some distinction on his breast, was sitting in his consulting-room that morning in his comfortable armchair. He was drinking coffee, which his wife had brought him with her own hand, smoking a cigar and from time to time writing prescriptions for his patients. After prescribing a draught for an old man who was suffering from hæmorrhoids and seeing the aged patient out by the side door, Krestyan Ivanovitch sat down to await the next visitor.

Mr. Golyadkin walked in.

Apparently Krestyan Ivanovitch did not in the least expect nor desire to see Mr. Golyadkin, for he was suddenly taken aback for a moment, and his countenance unconsciously assumed a strange and, one may almost say, a displeased expression. As Mr. Golyadkin almost always turned up inappropriately and was thrown into confusion whenever he approached any one about his own little affairs, on this occasion, too, he was desperately embarrassed. Having neglected to get ready his first sentence, which was invariably a stumbling-block for him on such occasions, he muttered something—apparently an apology—and, not knowing what to do next, took a chair and sat down, but, realizing that he had sat down without being asked to do so, he was immediately conscious of his lapse, and made haste to efface his offence against etiquette and good breeding by promptly getting up again from the seat he had taken uninvited. Then, on second thoughts, dimly perceiving that he had committed two stupid blunders at once, he immediately decided to commit a third—that is, tried to right himself, muttered something, smiled, blushed, was overcome with embarrassment, sank into expressive silence, and finally sat down for good and did not get up again. Only, to protect himself from all contingencies, he looked at the doctor with that defiant glare which had an extraordinary power of figuratively crushing Mr. Golyadkin's enemies and reducing them to ashes. This glance, moreover, expressed to the full Mr. Golyadkin's independence—that is, to speak plainly, the fact that Mr. Golyadkin was "all right," that he was "quite himself, like everybody else," and that there was "nothing wrong in his upper storey." Krestyan Ivanovitch coughed, cleared his throat, apparently in token of approval and assent to all this, and bent an inquisitorial interrogative gaze upon his visitor.

"I have come to trouble you a second time, Krestyan Ivanovitch," began Mr. Golyadkin, with a smile, "and now I venture to ask your indulgence a second time. . . ." He was obviously at a loss for words.

"H'm . . . Yes!" pronounced Krestyan Ivanovitch, puffing out a spiral of smoke and putting down his cigar on the table, "but you must follow the treatment prescribed you; I explained to you that what would be beneficial to your health is a change of habits. . . . Entertainment, for instance, and, well, friends—you should visit your acquaintances, and not be hostile to the bottle; and likewise keep cheerful company."

Mr. Golyadkin, still smiling, hastened to observe that he thought he was like every one else, that he lived by himself, that he had entertainments like every one else . . . that, of course, he might go to the theatre, for he had the means like every one else, that he spent the day at the office and the evenings at home, that he was quite all right; he even observed, in passing, that he was, so far as he could see, as good as any one, that he lived at home, and, finally, that he had Petrushka. At this point Mr. Golyadkin hesitated.

"H'm! no, that is not the order of proceeding I want; and that is not at all what I would ask you. I am interested to know, in general, are you a great lover of cheerful company? Do you take advantages of festive occasions; and, well, do you lead a melancholy or cheerful manner of life?"

"Krestyan Ivanovitch, I . . ."

"H'm! . . . I tell you," interrupted the doctor, "that you must have a radical change of life, must, in a certain sense, break in your character." (Krestyan Ivanovitch laid special stress on the word "break in," and paused for a moment with a very significant air.) "Must not shrink from gaiety, must visit entertainments and clubs, and in any case, be not hostile to the bottle. Sitting at home is not right for you . . . sitting at home is impossible for you."

"I like quiet, Krestyan Ivanovitch," said Mr. Golyadkin, with a significant look at the doctor and evidently seeking words to express his ideas more successfully: "In my flat there's only me and Petrushka. . . . I mean my man, Krestyan Ivanovitch. I mean to say, Krestyan Ivanovitch, that I go my way, my own way, Krestyan Ivanovitch. I keep myself to myself, and so far as I can see am not dependent on any one. I go out for walks, too, Krestyan Ivanovitch."

"What? Yes! well, nowadays there's nothing agreeable in walking: the climate's extremely bad."

"Quite so, Krestyan Ivanovitch. Though I'm a peaceable man, Krestyan Ivanovitch, as I've had the honour of explaining to you already, yet my way lies apart, Krestyan Ivanovitch. The ways of life are manifold. . . . I mean . . . I mean to say, Krestyan Ivanovitch. . . . Excuse me, Krestyan Ivanovitch, I've no great gift for eloquent speaking."

"H'm . . . you say . . ."

"I say, you must excuse me, Krestyan Ivanovitch, that as far as I can see I am no great hand at eloquence in speaking," Mr. Golyadkin articulated, stammering and hesitating, in a half-aggrieved voice. "In that respect, Krestyan Ivanovitch, I'm not quite like other people," he added, with a peculiar smile, "I can't talk much, and have never learnt to embellish my speech with literary graces. On the other hand, I act, Krestyan Ivanovitch; on the other hand, I act, Krestyan Ivanovitch."

"H'm . . . How's that . . . you act?" responded Krestyan Ivanovitch.

Then silence followed for half a minute. The doctor looked somewhat strangely and mistrustfully at his visitor. Mr. Golyadkin, for his part, too, stole a rather mistrustful glance at the doctor.

"Krestyan Ivanovitch," he began, going on again in the same tone as before, somewhat irritated and puzzled by the doctor's extreme obstinacy: "I like tranquillity and not the noisy gaiety of the world. Among them, I mean, in the noisy world, Krestyan Ivanovitch, one must be able to polish the floor with one's boots . . ." (here Mr. Golyadkin made a slight scrape on the floor with his toe); "they expect it, and they expect puns too . . . one must know how to make a perfumed compliment . . . that's what they expect there. And I've not learnt to do it, Krestyan Ivanovitch, I've never learnt all those tricks, I've never had the time. I'm a simple person, and not ingenious, and I've no external polish. On that side I surrender, Krestyan Ivanovitch, I lay down my arms, speaking in that sense."

All this Mr. Golyadkin pronounced with an air which made it perfectly clear that our hero was far from regretting that he was laying down his arms in that sense and that he had not learnt these tricks; quite the contrary, indeed. As Krestyan Ivanovitch listened to him, he looked down with a very unpleasant grimace on his face, seeming to have a presentiment of something. Mr. Golyadkin's tirade was followed by a rather long and significant silence.

"You have, I think, departed a little from the subject," Krestyan Ivanovitch said at last, in a low voice: "I confess I cannot altogether understand you."

"I'm not a great hand at eloquent speaking, Krestyan Ivanovitch; I've had the honour to inform you, Krestyan Ivanovitch, already," said Mr. Golyadkin, speaking this time in a sharp and resolute tone.

"H'm!" . . .

"Krestyan Ivanovitch!" began Mr. Golyadkin again in a low but more significant voice, in a somewhat solemn style and emphasizing every point: "Krestyan Ivanovitch, when I came in here I began with apologies. I repeat the same thing again, and again ask for your indulgence. There's no need for me to conceal it, Krestyan Ivanovitch. I'm an unimportant man, as you know; but, fortunately for me, I do not regret being an unimportant man. Quite the contrary, indeed, Krestyan Ivanovitch, and, to be perfectly frank, I'm proud that I'm not a great man but an unimportant man. I'm not one to intrigue and I'm proud of that too, I don't act on the sly, but openly, without cunning, and although I could do harm too, and a great deal of harm, indeed, and know to whom and how to do it, Krestyan Ivanovitch, yet I won't sully myself, and in that sense I wash my hands. In that sense, I say, I wash them, Krestyan Ivanovitch!" Mr. Golyadkin paused expressively for a moment; he spoke with mild fervour.

"I set to work, Krestyan Ivanovitch," our hero continued, "directly, openly, by no devious ways, for I disdain them, and leave them to others. I do not try to degrade those who are perhaps purer than you and I . . . that is, I mean, I and they, Krestyan Ivanovitch—I didn't mean you. I don't like insinuations; I've no taste for contemptible duplicity; I'm disgusted by slander and calumny. I only put on a mask at a masquerade, and don't wear one before people every day. I only ask you, Krestyan Ivanovitch, how you would revenge yourself upon your enemy, your most malignant enemy—the one you would consider such?" Mr. Golyadkin concluded with a challenging glance at Krestyan Ivanovitch.

Though Mr. Golyadkin pronounced this with the utmost distinctness and clearness, weighing his words with a self-confident air and reckoning on their probable effect, yet meanwhile he looked at Krestyan Ivanovitch with anxiety, with great anxiety, with extreme anxiety. Now he was all eyes: and timidly waited for the doctor's answer with irritable and agonized impatience. But to the perplexity and complete amazement of our hero, Krestyan Ivanovitch only muttered something to himself; then he moved his armchair up to the table, and rather drily though politely announced something to the effect that his time was precious, and that he did not quite understand; that he was ready, however, to attend to him as far as he was able, but he would not go into anything further that did not concern him. At this point he took the pen, drew a piece of paper towards him, cut out of it the usual long strip, and announced that he would immediately prescribe what was necessary.

"No, it's not necessary, Krestyan Ivanovitch! No, that's not necessary at all!" said Mr. Golyadkin, getting up from his seat, and clutching Krestyan Ivanovitch's right hand. "That isn't what's wanted, Krestyan Ivanovitch."

And, while he said this, a queer change came over him. His grey eyes gleamed strangely, his lips began to quiver, all the muscles, all the features of his face began moving and working. He was trembling all over. After stopping the doctor's hand, Mr. Golyadkin followed his first movement by standing motionless, as though he had no confidence in himself and were waiting for some inspiration for further action.

Then followed a rather strange scene.

Somewhat perplexed, Krestyan Ivanovitch seemed for a moment rooted to his chair and gazed open-eyed in bewilderment at Mr. Golyadkin, who looked at him in exactly the same way. At last Krestyan Ivanovitch stood up, gently holding the lining of Mr. Golyadkin's coat. For some seconds they both stood like that, motionless, with their eyes fixed on each other. Then, however, in an extraordinarily strange way came Mr. Golyadkin's second movement. His lips trembled, his chin began twitching, and our hero quite unexpectedly burst into tears. Sobbing, shaking his head and striking himself on the chest with his right hand, while with his left clutching the lining of the doctor's coat, he tried to say something and to make some explanation, but could not utter a word.

At last Krestyan Ivanovitch recovered from his amazement.

"Come, calm yourself!" he brought out at last, trying to make Mr. Golyadkin sit down in an armchair.

"I have enemies, Krestyan Ivanovitch, I have enemies; I have malignant enemies who have sworn to ruin me . . ." Mr. Golyadkin answered in a frightened whisper.

"Come, come, why enemies? you mustn't talk about enemies! You really mustn't. Sit down, sit down," Krestyan Ivanovitch went on, getting Mr. Golyadkin once for all into the armchair.

Mr. Golyadkin sat down at last, still keeping his eyes fixed on the doctor. With an extremely displeased air, Krestyan Ivanovitch strode from one end of the room to another. A long silence followed.

"I'm grateful to you, Krestyan Ivanovitch, I'm very grateful, and I'm very sensible of all you've done for me now. To my dying day I shall never forget your kindness, Krestyan Ivanovitch," said Mr. Golyadkin, getting up from his seat with an offended air.

"Come, give over! I tell you, give over!" Krestyan Ivanovitch responded rather sternly to Mr. Golyadkin's outburst, making him sit down again.

"Well, what's the matter? Tell me what is unpleasant," Krestyan Ivanovitch went on, "and what enemies are you talking about? What is wrong?"

"No, Krestyan Ivanovitch, we'd better leave that now," answered Mr. Golyadkin, casting down his eyes; "let us put all that aside for the time. . . . Till another time, Krestyan Ivanovitch, till a more convenient moment, when everything will be discovered and the mask falls off certain faces, and something comes to light. But, meanwhile, now, of course, after what has passed between us . . . you will agree yourself, Krestyan Ivanovitch. . . . Allow me to wish you good morning, Krestyan Ivanovitch," said Mr. Golyadkin, getting up gravely and resolutely and taking his hat.

"Oh, well . . . as you like . . . h'm . . ." (A moment of silence followed.) "For my part, you know . . . whatever I can do . . . and I sincerely wish you well."

"I understand you, Krestyan Ivanovitch, I understand: I understand you perfectly now . . . In any case excuse me for having troubled you, Krestyan Ivanovitch."

"H'm, no, I didn't mean that. However, as you please; go on taking the medicines as before. . . ."

"I will go on with the medicines as you say, Krestyan Ivanovitch. I will go on with them, and I will get them at the same chemist's . . . To be a chemist nowadays, Krestyan Ivanovitch, is an important business. . . ."

"How so? In what sense do you mean?"

"In a very ordinary sense, Krestyan Ivanovitch. I mean to say that nowadays that's the way of the world. . . ."

"H'm . . ."

"And that every silly youngster, not only a chemist's boy turns up his nose at respectable people."

"H'm. How do you understand that?"

"I'm speaking of a certain person, Krestyan Ivanovitch . . . of a common acquaintance of ours, Krestyan Ivanovitch, of Vladimir Semyonovitch. . . ."

"Ah!"

"Yes, Krestyan Ivanovitch: and I know certain people, Krestyan Ivanovitch, who don't quite keep to the general rule of telling the truth, sometimes."

"Ah! How so?"

"Why, yes, it is so: but that's neither here nor there: they sometimes manage to serve you up a fine egg in gravy."

"What? Serve up what?"

"An egg in gravy, Krestyan Ivanovitch. It's a Russian saying. They know how to congratulate some one at the right moment, for instance; there are people like that."

"Congratulate?"

"Yes, congratulate, Krestyan Ivanovitch, as some one I know very well did the other day!"

"Some one you know very well . . . Ah! how was that?" said Krestyan Ivanovitch, looking attentively at Mr. Golyadkin.

"Yes, some one I know very well indeed congratulated some one else I know very well—and, what's more, a comrade, a friend of his heart, on his promotion, on his receiving the rank of assessor. This was how it happened to come up: 'I am exceedingly glad of the opportunity to offer you, Vladimir Semyonovitch, my congratulations, my *sincere* congratulations, on your receiving the rank of assessor. And I'm the more pleased, as all the world knows that there are old women nowadays who tell fortunes.'"

At this point Mr. Golyadkin gave a sly nod, and screwing up his eyes, looked at Krestyan Ivanovitch. . . .

"H'm. So he said that. . . ."

"He did, Krestyan Ivanovitch, he said it and glanced at once at Andrey Filippovitch, the uncle of our Prince Charming, Vladimir Semyonovitch. But what is it to me, Krestyan Ivanovitch, that he has been made an assessor? What is it to me? And he wants to get married and the milk is scarcely dry on his lips, if I may be allowed the expression. And I said as much. Vladimir Semyonovitch, said I! I've said everything now; allow me to withdraw."

"H'm . . ."

"Yes, Krestyan Ivanovitch, allow me now, I say, to withdraw. But, to kill two birds with one stone, as I twitted our young gentleman with the old women, I turned to Klara Olsufyevna (it all happened the day before yesterday at Olsufy Ivanovitch's), and she had only just sung a song full of feeling, 'You've sung songs full of feeling, madam,' said I, 'but they've not been listened to with a pure heart.' And by that I hinted plainly, Krestyan Ivanovitch, hinted plainly, that they were not running after her now, but looking higher . . ."

"Ah! And what did he say?"

"He swallowed the pill, Krestyan Ivanovitch, as the saying is."

"H'm . . ."

"Yes, Krestyan Ivanovitch. To the old man himself, too, I said, 'Olsufy Ivanovitch,' said I, 'I know how much I'm indebted to you, I appreciate to the full all the kindness you've showered upon me from my childhood up. But open your eyes, Olsufy Ivanovitch,' I said. 'Look about you. I myself do things openly and aboveboard, Olsufy Ivanovitch.'"

"Oh, really!"

"Yes, Krestyan Ivanovitch. Really . . ."

"What did he say?"

"Yes, what, indeed, Krestyan Ivanovitch? He mumbled one thing and another, and 'I know you,' and that 'his Excellency was a benevolent man'—he rambled on. . . . But, there, you know! he's begun to be a bit shaky, as they say, with old age."

"Ah! so that's how it is now . . ."

"Yes, Krestyan Ivanovitch. And that's how we all are! Poor old man! He looks towards the grave, breathes incense, as they say, while they concoct a piece of womanish gossip and he listens to it; without him they wouldn't . . ."

"Gossip, you say?"

"Yes, Krestyan Ivanovitch, they've concocted a womanish scandal. Our bear, too, had a finger in it, and his nephew, our Prince Charming. They've joined hands with the old women and, of course, they've concocted the affair. Would you believe it? They plotted the murder of some one! . . ."

"The murder of some one?"

"Yes, Krestyan Ivanovitch, the moral murder of some one. They spread about . . . I'm speaking of a man I know very well."

Krestyan Ivanovitch nodded.

"They spread rumours about him . . . I confess I'm ashamed to repeat them, Krestyan Ivanovitch."

"H'm. . . ."

"They spread a rumour that he had signed a promise to marry though he was already engaged in another quarter . . . and would you believe it, Krestyan Ivanovitch, to whom?"

"Really?"

"To a cook, to a disreputable German woman from whom he used to get his dinners; instead of paying what he owed, he offered her his hand."

"Is that what they say?"

"Would you believe it, Krestyan Ivanovitch? A low German, a nasty, shameless German, Karolina Ivanovna, if you know . . ."

"I confess, for my part . . ."

"I understand you, Krestyan Ivanovitch, I understand, and for my part I feel it . . ."

"Tell me, please, where are you living now?"

"Where am I living now, Krestyan Ivanovitch?"

"Yes . . . I want . . . I believe, you used to live . . ."

"Yes, Krestyan Ivanovitch, I did, I used to. To be sure I lived!" answered Mr. Golyadkin, accompanying his words with a little laugh, and somewhat disconcerting Krestyan Ivanovitch by his answer.

"No, you misunderstood me; I meant to say . . ."

"I, too, meant to say, Krestyan Ivanovitch, I meant it too," Mr. Golyadkin continued, laughing. "But I've kept you far too long, Krestyan Ivanovitch. I hope you will allow me now, to wish you good morning."

"H'm. . . ."

"Yes, Krestyan Ivanovitch, I understand you; I fully understand you now," said our hero, with a slight flourish before Krestyan Ivanovitch. "And so permit me to wish you good morning. . . ."

At this point our hero made a scrape with the toe of his boot and walked out of the room, leaving Krestyan Ivanovitch in the utmost amazement. As he went down the doctor's stairs he smiled and rubbed his hands gleefully. On the steps, breathing the fresh air and feeling himself at liberty, he was certainly prepared to admit that he was the happiest of mortals, and thereupon to go straight to his office—when suddenly his carriage rumbled up to the door: he glanced at it and remembered everything. Petrushka was already opening the carriage door. Mr. Golyadkin was completely overwhelmed by a strong and unpleasant sensation. He blushed, as it were, for a moment. Something seemed to stab him. He was just about to raise his foot to the carriage step when he suddenly turned round and looked towards Krestyan Ivanovitch's window. Yes, it was so! Krestyan Ivanovitch was standing at the window, was stroking his whiskers with his right hand and staring with some curiosity at the hero of our story.

"That doctor is silly," thought Mr. Golyadkin, huddling out of sight in the carriage; "extremely silly. He may treat his patients all right, but still . . . he's as stupid as a post."

Mr. Golyadkin sat down, Petrushka shouted "Off!" and the carriage rolled towards Nevsky Prospect again.

CHAPTER III

ALL that morning was spent by Mr. Golyadkin in a strange bustle of activity. On reaching the Nevsky Prospect our hero told the driver to stop at the bazaar. Skipping out of his carriage, he ran to the Arcade, accompanied by Petrushka, and went straight to a shop where gold and silver articles were for sale. One could see from his very air that he was overwhelmed with business and had a terrible amount to do. Arranging to purchase a complete dinner- and tea-service for fifteen hundred roubles and including in the bargain for that sum a cigar-case of ingenious form and a silver shaving-set, and finally, asking the price of some other articles, useful and agreeable in their own way, he ended by promising to come without fail next day, or to send for his purchases the same day. He took the number of the shop, and listening attentively to the shop-keeper, who was very pressing for a small deposit, said that he should have it all in good time. After which he took leave of the amazed shop-keeper and, followed by a regular flock of shopmen, walked along the Arcade, continually looking round at Petrushka and diligently seeking out fresh shops. On the way he dropped into a money-changer's and changed all his big notes into small ones, and though he lost on the exchange, his pocket-book was considerably fatter, which evidently afforded him extreme satisfaction. Finally, he stopped at a shop for ladies' dress materials. Here, too, after deciding to purchase goods for a considerable sum, Mr. Golyadkin promised to come again, took the number of the shop and, on being asked for a deposit, assured the shopkeeper that "he should have a deposit too, all in good time." Then he visited several other shops, making purchases in each of them, asked the price of various things, sometimes arguing a long time with the shopkeeper, going out of the shop and returning two or three times— in fact he displayed exceptional activity. From the Arcade our hero went to a well-known furniture shop, where he ordered furniture for six rooms; he admired a fashionable and very ingenious toilet table for ladies' use in the latest style, and, assuring the shopkeeper that he would certainly send for all these things, walked out of the shop, as usual promising a deposit. Then he went off somewhere else and ordered something more. In short, there seemed to be no end to the business he had to get through. At last, Mr. Golyadkin seemed to grow heartily sick of it all, and he began, goodness knows why, to be tormented by the stings of conscience. Nothing would have induced him now, for instance, to meet Andrey Filippovitch, or even Krestyan Ivanovitch.

At last, the town clock struck three. When Mr. Golyadkin finally took his seat in the carriage, of all the purchases he had made that morning he had, it appeared, in reality only got a pair of gloves and a bottle of scent, that cost a rouble and a half. As it was still rather early, he ordered his coachman to stop near a well-known restaurant in Nevsky Prospect which he only knew by reputation, got out of the carriage, and hurried in to have a light lunch, to rest and to wait for the hour fixed for the dinner.

Lunching as a man lunches who has the prospect before him of going out to a sumptuous dinner, that is, taking a snack of something in order to still the pangs, as they say, and drinking one small glass of vodka, Mr. Golyadkin established himself in an armchair and, modestly looking about him, peacefully settled down to an emaciated nationalist paper. After reading a couple of lines he stood up and looked in the looking-glass, set himself to rights and smoothed himself down; then he went to the window and looked to see whether his carriage was there . . . then he sat down again in his place and took up the paper. It was noticeable that our hero was in great excitement. Glancing at his watch and seeing that it was only a quarter past three and that he had consequently a good time to wait and, at the same time, opining that to sit like that was unsuitable, Mr. Golyadkin ordered chocolate, though he felt no particular inclination for it at the moment. Drinking the chocolate and noticing that the time had moved on a little, he went up to pay his bill.

He turned round and saw facing him two of his colleagues, the same two he had met that morning in Liteyny Street,—young men, very much his juniors both in age and in rank. Our hero's relations with them were neither one thing nor the other, neither particularly friendly nor openly hostile. Good manners were, of course, observed on both sides: there was no closer intimacy, nor could there be. The meeting at this moment was extremely distasteful to Mr. Golyadkin. He frowned a little, and was disconcerted for an instant.

"Yakov Petrovitch, Yakov Petrovitch!" chirped the two register clerks; "you here? what brings you? . . ."

"Ah, it is you, gentlemen," Mr. Golyadkin interrupted hurriedly, somewhat embarrassed and scandalized by the amazement of the clerks and by the abruptness of their address, but feeling obliged, however, to appear jaunty and free and easy. "You've deserted, gentlemen, he—he—he. . . ." Then, to keep up his dignity and to condescend to the juveniles, with whom he never overstepped certain limits, he attempted to slap one of the youths on the shoulder; but this effort at good fellowship did not succeed and, instead of being a well-bred little jest, produced quite a different effect.

"Well, and our bear, is he still at the office?"

"Who's that, Yakov Petrovitch?"

"Why, the bear. Do you mean to say you don't know whose name that is? . . ." Mr. Golyadkin laughed and turned to the cashier to take his change.

"I mean Andrey Filippovitch, gentlemen," he went on, finishing with the cashier, and turning to the clerks this time with a very serious face. The two register clerks winked at one another.

"He's still at the office and asking for you, Yakov Petrovitch," answered one of them.

"At the office, eh! In that case, let him stay, gentlemen. And asking for me, eh?"

"He was asking for you, Yakov Petrovitch; but what's up with you, scented, pomaded, and such a swell? . . ."

"Nothing, gentlemen, nothing! that's enough," answered Mr. Golyadkin, looking away with a constrained smile. Seeing that Mr. Golyadkin was smiling, the clerks laughed aloud. Mr. Golyadkin was a little offended.

"I'll tell you as friends, gentlemen," our hero said, after a brief silence, as though making up his mind (which, indeed, was the case) to reveal something to them. "You all know me, gentlemen, but hitherto you've known me only on one side. No one is to blame for that and I'm conscious that the fault has been partly my own."

Mr. Golyadkin pursed up his lips and looked significantly at the clerks. The clerks winked at one another again.

"Hitherto, gentlemen, you have not known me. To explain myself here and now would not be quite appropriate. I will only touch on it lightly in passing. There are people, gentlemen, who dislike roundabout ways and only mask themselves at masquerades. There are people who do not see man's highest avocation in polishing the floor with their boots. There are people, gentlemen, who refuse to say that they are happy and enjoying a full life when, for instance, their trousers set properly. There are people, finally, who dislike dashing and whirling about for no object, fawning, and licking the dust, and above all, gentlemen, poking their noses where they are not wanted . . . I've told you almost everything, gentlemen; now allow me to withdraw. . . ."

Mr. Golyadkin paused. As the register clerks had now got all that they wanted, both of them with great incivility burst into shouts of laughter. Mr. Golyadkin flared up.

"Laugh away, gentlemen, laugh away for the time being! If you live long enough you will see," he said, with a feeling of offended dignity, taking his hat and retreating to the door.

"But I will say more, gentlemen," he added, turning for the last time to the register clerks, "I will say more—you are both here with me face to face. This, gentlemen, is my rule: if I fail I don't lose heart, if I succeed I persevere, and in any case I am never underhand. I'm not one to intrigue—and I'm proud of it. I've never prided myself on diplomacy. They say, too, gentlemen, that the bird flies itself to the hunter. It's true and I'm ready to admit it; but who's the hunter, and who's the bird in this case? That is still the question, gentlemen!"

Mr. Golyadkin subsided into eloquent silence, and, with a most significant air, that is, pursing up his lips and raising his eyebrows as high as possible, he bowed to the clerks and walked out, leaving them in the utmost amazement.

"What are your orders now?" Petrushka asked, rather gruffly; he was probably weary of hanging about in the cold. "What are your orders?" he asked Mr. Golyadkin, meeting the terrible, withering glance with which our hero had protected himself twice already that morning, and to which he had recourse now for the third time as he came down the steps.

"To Ismailovsky Bridge."

"To Ismailovsky Bridge! Off!"

"Their dinner will not begin till after four, or perhaps five o'clock," thought Mr. Golyadkin; "isn't it early now? However, I can go a little early; besides, it's only a family dinner. And so I can go *sans façons,* as they say among well-bred people. Why shouldn't I go *sans façons?* The bear told us, too, that it would all be *san façons,* and so I will be the same. . . ." Such were Mr. Golyadkin's reflections and meanwhile his excitement grew more and more acute. It could be seen that he was preparing himself for some great enterprise, to say nothing more; he muttered to himself, gesticulated with his right hand, continually looked out of his carriage window, so that, looking at Mr. Golyadkin, no one would have said that he was on his way to a good dinner, and only a simple dinner in his family circle—*sans façons,* as they say among well-bred people. Finally, just at Ismailovsky Bridge, Mr. Golyadkin pointed out a house; and the carriage rolled up noisily and stopped at the first entrance on the right. Noticing a feminine figure at the second storey window, Mr. Golyadkin kissed his hand to her. He had, however, not the slightest idea what he was doing, for he felt more dead than alive at the moment. He got out of the carriage pale, distracted; he mounted the steps, took off his hat, mechanically straightened himself, and though he felt a slight trembling in his knees, he went upstairs.

"Olsufy Ivanovitch?" he inquired of the man who opened the door.

"At home, sir; at least he's not at home, his honour's not at home."

"What? What do you mean, my good man? I—I've come to dinner, brother. Why, you know me?"

"To be sure I know you! I've orders not to admit you."

"You . . . you, brother . . . you must be making a mistake. It's I, my boy, I'm invited; I've come to dinner," Mr. Golyadkin announced, taking off his coat and displaying unmistakable intentions of going into the room.

"Allow me, sir, you can't, sir. I've orders not to admit you. I've orders to refuse you. That's how it is."

Mr. Golyadkin turned pale. At that very moment the door of the inner room opened and Gerasimitch, Olsufy Ivanovitch's old butler, came out.

"You see the gentleman wants to go in, Emelyan Gerasimitch, and I . . ."

"And you're a fool, Alexeitch. Go inside and send the rascal Semyonitch here. It's impossible," he said politely but firmly, addressing Mr. Golyadkin. "It's quite impossible. His honour begs you to excuse him; he can't see you."

"He said he couldn't see me?" Mr. Golyadkin asked uncertainly. "Excuse me, Gerasimitch, why is it impossible?"

"It's quite impossible. I've informed your honour; they said 'Ask him to excuse us.' They can't see you."

"Why not? How's that? Why."

"Allow me, allow me! . . ."

"How is it, though? It's out of the question! Announce me. . . . How is it? I've come to dinner. . . ."

"Excuse me, excuse me. . . ."

"Ah, well, that's a different matter, they asked to be excused: but, allow me, Gerasimitch; how is it, Gerasimitch?"

"Excuse me, excuse me!" replied Gerasimitch, very firmly putting away Mr. Golyadkin's hand and making way for two gentlemen who walked into the entry that very instant. The gentlemen in question were Andrey Filippovitch and his nephew, Vladimir Semyonovitch. Both of them looked with amazement at Mr. Golyadkin. Andrey Filippovitch seemed about to say something, but Mr. Golyadkin had by now made up his mind: he was by now walking out of Olsufy Ivanovitch's entry, blushing and smiling, with eyes cast down and a countenance of helpless bewilderment. "I will come afterwards, Gerasimitch; I will explain myself: I hope that all this will without delay be explained in due season. . . ."

"Yakov Petrovitch, Yakov Petrovitch . . ." He heard the voice of Andrey Filippovitch following him.

Mr. Golyadkin was by that time on the first landing. He turned quickly to Andrey Filippovitch.

"What do you desire, Andrey Filippovitch?" he said in a rather resolute voice.

"What's wrong with you, Yakov Petrovitch? In what way?"

"No matter, Andrey Filippovitch. I'm on my own account here. This is my private life, Andrey Filippovitch."

"What's that?"

"I say, Andrey Filippovitch, that this is my private life, and as for my being here, as far as I can see, there's nothing reprehensible to be found in it as regards my official relations."

"What! As regards your official . . . What's the matter with you, my good sir?"

"Nothing, Andrey Filippovitch, absolutely nothing; an impudent slut of a girl, and nothing more. . . ."

"What! What?" Andrey Filippovitch was stupefied with amazement. Mr. Golyadkin, who had up till then looked as though he would fly into

Andrey Filippovitch's face, seeing that the head of his office was laughing a little, almost unconsciously took a step forward. Andrey Filippovitch jumped back. Mr. Golyadkin went up one step and then another. Andrey Filippovitch looked about him uneasily. Mr. Golyadkin mounted the stairs rapidly. Still more rapidly Andrey Filippovitch darted into the flat and slammed the door after him. Mr. Golyadkin was left alone. Everything grew dark before his eyes. He was utterly nonplussed, and stood now in a sort of senseless hesitation, as though recalling something extremely senseless, too, that had happened quite recently. "Ech, ech!" he muttered, smiling with constraint. Meanwhile, there came the sounds of steps and voices on the stairs, probably of other quests invited by Olsufy Ivanovitch. Mr. Golyadkin recovered himself to some extent; put up his raccoon collar, concealing himself behind it as far as possible, and began going downstairs with rapid little steps, tripping and stumbling in his haste. He felt overcome by a sort of weakness and numbness. His confusion was such that, when he came out on the steps, he did not even wait for his carriage but walked across the muddy court to it. When he reached his carriage and was about to get into it, Mr. Golyadkin inwardly uttered a desire to sink into the earth, or to hide in a mouse hole together with his carriage. It seemed to him that everything in Olsufy Ivanovitch's house was looking at him now out of every window. He knew that he would certainly die on the spot if he were to go back.

"What are you laughing at, blockhead?" he said in a rapid mutter to Petrushka, who was preparing to help him into the carriage.

"What should I laugh at? I'm not doing anything; where are we to drive now?"

"Go home, drive on. . . ."

"Home, off!" shouted Petrushka, climbing on to the footboard.

"What a crow's croak!" thought Mr. Golyadkin. Meanwhile, the carriage had driven a good distance from Ismailovsky Bridge. Suddenly our hero pulled the cord with all his might and shouted to the driver to turn back at once. The coachman turned his horses and within two minutes was driving into Olsufy Ivanovitch's yard again.

"Don't, don't, you fool, back!" shouted Mr. Golyadkin—and, as though he were expecting this order, the driver made no reply but, without stopping at the entrance, drove all round the courtyard and out into the street again.

Mr. Golyadkin did not drive home, but, after passing the Semyonovsky Bridge, told the driver to return to a side street and stop near a restaurant of rather modest appearance. Getting out of the carriage, our hero settled up with the driver and so got rid of his equipage at last. He told Petrushka to go home and await his return, while he went into the restaurant, took a private room and ordered dinner. He felt very ill and his brain was in the utmost confusion and chaos. For a long time he walked up and down the room in agitation; at last he sat down in a chair, propped his brow in his hands and began doing his very utmost to consider and settle something relating to his present position.

CHAPTER IV

THAT day the birthday of Klara Olsufyevna, the only daughter of the civil councillor, Berendyev, at one time Mr. Golyadkin's benefactor and patron, was being celebrated by a brilliant and sumptuous dinner-party, such as had not been seen for many a long day within the walls of the flats in the neighbourhood of Ismailovsky Bridge—a dinner more like some Balthazar's feast, with a suggestion of something Babylonian in its brilliant luxury and style, with Veuve-Clicquot champagne, with oysters and fruit from Eliseyev's and Milyutin's, with all sorts of fatted calves, and all grades of the government service. This festive day was to conclude with a brilliant ball, a small birthday ball, but yet brilliant in its taste, its distinction and its style. Of course, I am willing to admit that similar balls do happen sometimes, though rarely. Such balls, more like family rejoicings than balls, can only be given in such houses as that of the civil councillor, Berendyev. I will say more: I even doubt if such balls could be given in the houses of all civil councillors. Oh, if I were a poet! such as Homer or Pushkin, I mean, of course; with any lesser talent one would not venture—I should certainly have painted all that glorious day for you, oh, my readers, with a free brush and brilliant colours! Yes, I should begin my poem with my dinner, I should lay special stress on that striking and solemn moment when the first goblet was raised to the honour of the queen of the fête. I should describe to you the guests plunged in a reverent silence and expectation, as eloquent as the rhetoric of Demosthenes; I should describe for you, then, how Andrey Filippovitch, having as the eldest of the guests some right to take precedence, adorned with his grey hairs and the orders that well befit grey hairs, got up from his seat and raised above his head the congratulatory glass of sparkling wine—brought from a distant kingdom to celebrate such occasions and more like heavenly nectar than plain wine. I would portray for you the guests and the happy parents raising their glasses, too, after Andrey Filippovitch, and fastening upon him eyes full of expectation. I would describe for you how the same Andrey Filippovitch, so often mentioned, after dropping a tear in the glass, delivered his congratulations and good wishes, proposed the toast and drank the health . . . but I confess, I freely confess, that I could not do justice to the solemn moment when the queen of the fête, Klara Olsuf-yevna, blushing like a rose in spring, with the glow of bliss and of modesty, was so overcome by her feelings that she sank into the arms of her tender mamma; how that tender mamma shed tears, and how the father, Olsufy Ivanovitch, a hale old man and a privy councillor, who had lost the use of his legs in his long years of service and been reward-ed by destiny for his devotion with investments, a house, some small estates, and a beautiful daughter, sobbed like a little child and announced through his tears that his Excellency was a benevolent man. I could not, I positively could not, describe the enthusiasm that fol-lowed that moment in every heart, an enthusiasm clearly evinced in the conduct of a youthful register clerk (though at that moment he was more like a civil councillor than a register clerk), who was moved to tears, too, as he listened to Andrey Filippovitch. In his turn, too, Andrey Filippovitch was in that solemn moment quite unlike a collegiate coun-cillor and the head of an office in the department—yes, he was some-thing else . . . what, exactly, I do not know, but not a collegiate coun-cillor. He was more exalted! Finally . . . Oh, why do I not possess the secret of lofty, powerful language, of the sublime style, to describe these grand and edifying moments of human life, which seem created expressly to prove that virtue sometimes triumphs over ingratitude, free-thinking, vice and envy! I will say nothing, but in silence—which will be better than any eloquence—I will point to that fortunate youth, just entering on his twenty-sixth spring—to Vladimir Semyonovitch, Andrey Filippovitch's nephew, who in his turn now rose from his seat, who in his turn proposed a toast, and upon whom were fastened the tearful eyes of the parents, the proud eyes of Andrey Filippovitch, the modest eyes of the queen of the fête, the solemn eyes of the guests, and even the decorously envious eyes of some of the young man's youthful colleagues. I will say nothing of that, though I cannot refrain from observing that everything in that young man—who was, indeed, speak-ing in a complimentary sense, more like an elderly than a young man—everything, from his blooming cheeks to his assessorial rank seemed almost to proclaim aloud the lofty pinnacle a man can attain through morality and good principles! I will not describe how Anton Antonovitch Syetotchkin, a little old man as grey as a badger, the head clerk of a department, who was a colleague of Andrey Filippovitch's and had once been also of Olsufy Ivanovitch's, and was an old friend of the family and Klara Olsufyevna's godfather, in his turn proposed a toast, crowed like a cock, and cracked many little jokes; how by this extremely proper breach of propriety, if one may use such an expression, he made the whole company laugh till they cried, and how Klara Olsufyevna, at her parents' bidding, rewarded him for his jocularity and politeness with a kiss. I will only say that the guests, who must have felt like kinsfolk and brothers after such a dinner, at last rose from the table, and the elderly and more solid guests, after a brief interval spent in friendly conversation, interspersed with some candid, though, of course, very polite and proper observations, went decorously into the next room and, without losing valuable time, promptly divided themselves up into parties and, full of the sense of their own dignity, installed themselves at tables covered with green baize. Meanwhile, the ladies established in the drawing-room suddenly became very affable and began talking about dress-materials. And the venerable host, who had lost the use of his legs in the service of loyalty and religion, and had been rewarded with all the blessings we have enumerated above, began walking about on crutches among his guests, supported by Vladimir Semyonovitch and Klara Olsufyevna, and he, too, suddenly becoming extremely affable, decided to improvise a modest little dance, regardless of expense; to that end a nimble youth (the one who was more like a civil councillor than a youth) was despatched to fetch musicians, and musicians to the number of eleven arrived, and exactly at half-past eight struck up the inviting strains of a French quadrille, followed by various other dances. . . . It is needless to say that my pen is too weak, dull, and spiritless to describe the dance that owed its inspiration to the genial hospitality of the grey-headed host. And how, I ask, can the modest chronicler of Mr. Golyadkin's adventures, extremely interesting as they are in their own way, how can I depict the choice and rare mingling of beauty, brilliance, style, gaiety, polite solidity and solid politeness, sportiveness, joy, all the mirth and playfulness of these wives and daughters of petty officials, more like fairies than ladies — in a complimentary sense — with their lily shoulders and their rosy faces, their ethereal figures, their playfully agile homeopathic — to use the exalted language appropriate — little feet? How can I describe to you, finally, the gallant officials, their partners — gay and solid youths, steady, gleeful, decorously vague, smoking a pipe in the intervals between the dancing in a little green room apart, or not smoking a pipe in the intervals between the dances, every one of them with a highly respectable surname and rank in the service—all steeped in a sense of the elegant and a sense of their own dignity; almost all speaking French to their partners, or if Russian, using only the most well-bred expressions, compliments and profound observations, and only in the smoking-room permitting themselves some genial lapses from this high tone, some phrases of cordial and friendly brevity, such, for instance, as: "'Pon my soul, Petka, you rake, you did kick off that polka in style," or, "I say, Vasya, you dog, you did give your partner a time of it." For all this, as I've already had the honour of explaining, oh, my readers! my pen fails me, and therefore I am dumb. Let us rather return to Mr. Golyadkin, the true and only hero of my very truthful tale.

The fact is that he found himself now in a very strange position, to say the least of it. He was here also, gentlemen—that is, not at the dance, but almost at the dance; he was "all right, though; he could take care of himself," yet at this moment he was a little astray; he was standing at that moment, strange to say—on the landing of the back stairs to Olsufy Ivanovitch's flat. But it was "all right" his standing there; he was "quite well." He was standing in a corner, huddled in a place which was not very warm, though it was dark, partly hidden by a huge cupboard and an old screen, in the midst of rubbish, litter, and odds and ends of all sorts, concealing himself for the time being and watching the course of proceedings as a disinterested spectator. He was only looking on now, gentlemen; he, too, gentlemen, might go in, of course . . . why should he not go in? He had only to take one step and he would go in, and would go in very adroitly. Just now, though he had been standing nearly three hours between the cupboard and the screen in the midst of the rubbish, litter, and odds and ends of all sorts, he was only quoting, in his own justification, a memorable phrase of the French minister, Villesle: "All things come in time to him who has the strength to wait." Mr. Golyadkin had read this sentence in some book on quite a different subject, but now very aptly recalled it. The phrase, to begin with, was exceedingly appropriate to his present position, and, indeed, why should it not occur to the mind of a man who had been waiting for almost three hours in the cold and the dark in expectation of a happy ending to his adventures. After quoting very appropriately the phrase of the French minister, Villesle, Mr. Golyadkin immediately thought of the Turkish Vizier, Martsimiris, as well as of the beautiful Margravine Luise, whose story he had read also in some book. Then it occurred to his mind that the Jesuits made it their rule that any means were justified if only the end were attained. Fortifying himself somewhat with this historical fact, Mr. Golyadkin said to himself, What were the

Jesuits? The Jesuits were every one of them very great fools; that he was better than any of them; that if only the refreshment-room would be empty for one minute (the door of the refreshment-room opened straight into the passage to the back stairs, where Mr. Golyadkin was in hiding now), he would, in spite of all the Jesuits in the world, go straight in, first from the refreshment-room into the tea-room, then into the room where they were now playing cards, and then straight into the hall where they were now dancing the polka, and he would go in, he would certainly go in, in spite of anything he would go in—he would slip through—and that would be all, no one would notice him; and once there he would know what to do.

Well, so this is the position in which we find the hero of our perfectly true story, though, indeed, it is difficult to explain what was passing in him at that moment. The fact is that he had made his way to the back stairs and to the passage, on the ground that, as he said, "why shouldn't he? and everyone did go that way"; but he had not ventured to penetrate further, evidently he did not dare to do so . . . "not because there was anything he did not dare, but just because he did not care to, because he preferred to be in hiding"; so here he was, waiting now for a chance to slip in, and he had been waiting for it two hours and a half. "Why not wait? Villesle himself had waited. But what had Villesle to do with it?" thought Mr. Golyadkin: "How does Villesle come in? But how am I to . . . to go and walk in? . . . Ech, you dummy!" said Mr. Golyadkin, pinching his benumbed cheek with his benumbed fingers; "you silly fool, you silly old Golyadkin—silly fool of a surname! . . ."

But these compliments paid to himself were only by the way and without any apparent aim. Now he was on the point of pushing forward and slipping in; the refreshment-room was empty and no one was in sight. Mr. Golyadkin saw all this through the little window; in two steps he was at the door and had already opened it. "Should he go in or not? Come, should he or not? I'll go in . . . why not? to the bold all ways lie open!" Reassuring himself in this way, our hero suddenly and quite unexpectedly retreated behind the screen. "No," he thought. "Ah, now, somebody's coming in? Yes, they've come in; why did I dawdle when there were no people about? Even so, shall I go and slip in? . . . No, how slip in when a man has such a temperament! Fie, what a low tendency! I'm as scared as a hen! Being scared is our special line, that's the fact of the matter! To be abject on every occasion is our line: no need to ask us about that. Just stand here like a post and that's all! At home I should be having a cup of tea now. . . . It would be pleasant, too, to have a cup of tea. If I come in later Petrushka 'll grumble, maybe. Shall I go home?

Damnation take all this! I'll go and that 'll be the end of it!" Reflecting on his position in this way, Mr. Golyadkin dashed forward as though some one had touched a spring in him; in two steps he found himself in the refreshment-room, flung off his overcoat, took off his hat, hurriedly thrust these things into a corner, straightened himself and smoothed himself down; then . . . then he moved on to the tea-room, and from the tea-room darted into the next room, slipped almost unnoticed between the card-players, who were at the tip-top of excitement, then . . . Mr. Golyadkin forgot everything that was going on about him, and went straight as an arrow into the drawing-room.

As luck would have it they were not dancing. The ladies were promenading up and down the room in picturesque groups. The gentlemen were standing about in twos and threes or flitting about the room engaging partners. Mr. Golyadkin noticed nothing of this. He saw only Klara Olsufyevna, near her Andrey Filippovitch, then Vladimir Semyonovitch, two or three officers, and, finally, two or three other young men who were also very interesting and, as any one could see at once, were either very promising or had actually done something. . . . He saw some one else too. Or, rather, he saw nobody and looked at nobody . . . but, moved by the same spring which had sent him dashing into the midst of a ball to which he had not been invited, he moved forward, and then forwarder and forwarder. On the way he jostled against a councillor and trod on his foot, and incidentally stepped on a very venerable old lady's dress and tore it a little, pushed against a servant with a tray and then ran against somebody else, and, not noticing all this, or rather noticing it but at the same time looking at no one, passing further and further forward, he suddenly found himself facing Klara Olsufyevna. There is no doubt whatever that he would, with the utmost delight, without winking an eyelid, have sunk through the earth at that moment; but what has once been done cannot be recalled . . . can never be recalled. What was he to do? "If I fail I don't lose heart, if I succeed I persevere." Mr. Golyadkin was, of course, not "one to intrigue," and "not accomplished in the art of polishing the floor with his boots." . . . And so, indeed, it proved. Besides, the Jesuits had some hand in it too . . . though Mr. Golyadkin had no thoughts to spare for them now! All the moving, noisy, talking, laughing groups were suddenly hushed as though at a signal and, little by little, crowded round Mr. Golyadkin. He, however, seemed to hear nothing, to see nothing, he could not look . . . he could not possibly look at anything; he kept his eyes on the floor and so stood, giving himself his word of honour, in passing, to shoot himself one way or another that night. Making this vow, Mr.

Golyadkin inwardly said to himself, "Here goes!" and to his own great astonishment began unexpectedly to speak.

He began with congratulations and polite wishes. The congratulations went off well, but over the good wishes our hero stammered. He felt that if he stammered all would be lost at once. And so it turned out—he stammered and floundered . . . floundering, he blushed crimson; blushing, he was overcome with confusion. In his confusion he raised his eyes; raising his eyes he looked about him; looking about him—he almost swooned. . . . Every one stood still, every one was silent, every one was waiting; a little way off there was whispering; a little nearer there was laughter. Mr. Golyadkin fastened a humble, imploring look on Andrey Filippovitch. Andrey Filippovitch responded with such a look that if our hero had not been utterly crushed already he certainly would have been crushed a second time—that is, if that were possible. The silence lasted long.

"This is rather concerned with my domestic circumstances and my private life, Andrey Filippovitch," our hero, half-dead, articulated in a scarcely audible voice; "it is not an official incident, Andrey Filippovitch . . ."

"For shame, sir, for shame!" Andrey Filippovitch pronounced in a half whisper, with an indescribable air of indignation; he pronounced these words and, giving Klara Olsufyevna his arm, he turned away from Mr. Golyadkin.

"I've nothing to be ashamed of, Andrey Filippovitch," answered Mr. Golyadkin, also in a whisper, turning his miserable eyes about him, trying helplessly to discover in the amazed crowd something on which he could gain a footing and retrieve his social position.

"Why, it's all right, it's nothing, gentlemen! Why, what's the matter? Why, it might happen to any one," whispered Mr. Golyadkin, moving a little away and trying to escape from the crowd surrounding him.

They made way for him. Our hero passed through two rows of inquisitive and wondering spectators. Fate drew him on. He felt that himself, that fate was leading him on. He would have given a great deal, of course, for a chance to be back in the passage by the back stairs, without having committed a breach of propriety; but as that was utterly impossible he began trying to creep away into a corner and to stand there—modestly, decorously, apart, without interfering with any one, without attracting especial attention, but at the same time to win the favourable notice of his host and the company. At the same time Mr. Golyadkin felt as though the ground were giving way under him, as though he were staggering, falling. At last he made his way to a corner

and stood in it, like an unconcerned, rather indifferent spectator, leaning his arms on the backs of two chairs, taking complete possession of
them in that way, and trying, as far as he could, to glance confidently at
Olsufy Ivanovitch's guests, grouped about him. Standing nearest him
was an officer, a tall and handsome fellow, beside whom Golyadkin felt
himself an insect.

"These two chairs, lieutenant, are intended, one for Klara Olsufyevna, and the other for Princess Tchevtchehanov; I'm taking care of
them for them," said Mr. Golyadkin breathlessly, turning his imploring eyes on the officer. The lieutenant said nothing, but turned away
with a murderous smile. Checked in this direction, our hero was about
to try his luck in another quarter, and directly addressed an important
councillor with a cross of great distinction on his breast. But the councillor looked him up and down with such a frigid stare that Mr.
Golyadkin felt distinctly as though a whole bucketful of cold water
had been thrown over him. He subsided into silence. He made up his
mind that it was better to keep quiet, not to open his lips, and to show
that he was "all right," that he was "like every one else," and that his
position, as far as he could see, was quite a proper one. With this
object he riveted his gaze on the lining of his coat, then raised his eyes
and fixed them upon a very respectable-looking gentleman. "That
gentleman has a wig on," thought Mr. Golyadkin; "and if he takes off
that wig he will be bald, his head will be as bare as the palm of my
hand." Having made this important discovery, Mr. Golyadkin thought
of the Arab Emirs, whose heads are left bare and shaven if they take
off the green turbans they wear as a sign of their descent from the
prophet Mahomet. Then, probably from some special connection of
ideas with the Turks, he thought of Turkish slippers and at once, apropos of that, recalled the fact that Andrey Filippovitch was wearing
boots, and that his boots were more like slippers than boots. It was evident that Mr. Golyadkin had become to some extent reconciled to his
position. "What if that chandelier," flashed through Mr. Golyadkin's
mind, "were to come down from the ceiling and fall upon the company. I should rush at once to save Klara Olsufyevna. 'Save her!' I
should cry. 'Don't be alarmed, madam, it's of no consequence, I will
rescue you, I.' Then . . ." At that moment Mr. Golyadkin looked about
in search of Klara Olsufyevna, and saw Gerasimitch, Olsufy
Ivanovitch's old butler. Gerasimitch, with a most anxious and solemnly official air, was making straight for him. Mr. Golyadkin started and
frowned from an unaccountable but most disagreeable sensation; he
looked about him mechanically; it occurred to his mind if only he

could somehow creep off somewhere, unobserved, on the sly—simply disappear, that is, behave as though he had done nothing at all, as though the matter did not concern him in the least! . . . But before our hero could make up his mind to do anything Gerasimitch was standing before him.

"Do you see, Gerasimitch," said our hero, with a little smile, addressing Gerasimitch; "you go and tell them—do you see the candle there in the chandelier, Gerasimitch—it will be falling down directly: so, you know, you must tell them to see it; it really will fall down, Gerasimitch. . . ."

"The candle? No, the candle's standing straight; but somebody is asking for you, sir."

"Who is asking for me, Gerasimitch?"

"I really can't say, sir, who it is. A man with a message. 'Is Yakov Petrovitch Golyadkin here?' says he. 'Then call him out,' says he, 'on very urgent and important business . . .' you see."

"No, Gerasimitch, you are making a mistake; in that you are making a mistake, Gerasimitch."

"I doubt it, sir."

"No, Gerasimitch, it isn't doubtful; there's nothing doubtful about it, Gerasimitch. Nobody's asking for me, but I'm quite at home here—that is, in my right place, Gerasimitch."

Mr. Golyadkin took breath and looked about him. Yes! every one in the room, all had their eyes fixed upon him, and were listening in a sort of solemn expectation. The men had crowded a little nearer and were all attention. A little further away the ladies were whispering together. The master of the house made his appearance at no great distance from Mr. Golyadkin, and though it was impossible to detect from his expression that he, too, was taking a close and direct interest in Mr. Golyadkin's position, for everything was being done with delicacy, yet, nevertheless, it all made our hero feel that the decisive moment had come for him. Mr. Golyadkin saw clearly that the time had come for a bold stroke, the chance of putting his enemies to shame. Mr. Golyadkin was in great agitation. He was aware of a sort of inspiration and, in a quivering and impressive voice, he began again, addressing the waiting butler—

"No, my dear fellow, no one's calling for me. You are mistaken. I will say more: you were mistaken this morning, too, when you assured me. . . . dared to assure me, I say" (he raised his voice), "that Olsufy Ivanovitch, who had been my benefactor as long as I can remember and has, in a sense, been a father to me, was shutting his door upon me at the moment of solemn family rejoicing for his paternal heart." (Mr.

Golyadkin looked about him complacently, but with deep feeling. A tear glittered on his eyelash.) "I repeat, my friend," our hero concluded, "you were mistaken, you were cruelly and unpardonably mistaken. . . ."

The moment was a solemn one. Mr. Golyadkin felt that the effect was quite certain. He stood with modestly downcast eyes, expecting Olsufy Ivanovitch to embrace him. Excitement and perplexity were apparent in the guests, even the inflexible and terrible Gerasimitch faltered over the words "I doubt it . . ." when suddenly the ruthless orchestra, apropos of nothing, struck up a polka. All was lost, all was scattered to the winds. Mr. Golyadkin started; Gerasimitch stepped back; everything in the room began undulating like the sea; and Vladimir Semyonovitch led the dance with Klara Olsufyevna, while the handsome lieutenant followed with Princess Tchevtchehanov. Onlookers, curious and delighted, squeezed in to watch them dancing the polka—an interesting, fashionable new dance which every one was crazy over. Mr. Golyadkin was, for the time, forgotten. But suddenly all were thrown into excitement, confusion and bustle; the music ceased . . . a strange incident had occurred. Tired out with the dance, and almost breathless with fatigue, Klara Olsufyevna, with glowing cheeks and heaving bosom, sank into an armchair, completely exhausted. . . . All hearts turned to the fascinating creature, all vied with one another in complimenting her and thanking her for the pleasure conferred on them,—all at once there stood before her Mr. Golyadkin. He was pale, extremely perturbed; he, too, seemed completely exhausted, he could scarcely move. He was smiling for some reason, he stretched out his hand imploringly. Klara Olsufyevna was so taken aback that she had not time to withdraw hers and mechanically got up at his invitation. Mr. Golyadkin lurched forward, first once, then a second time, then lifted his leg, then made a scrape, then gave a sort of stamp, then stumbled . . . he, too, wanted to dance with Klara Olsufyevna. Klara Olsufyevna uttered a shriek; every one rushed to release her hand from Mr. Golyadkin's, and in a moment our hero was carried almost ten paces away by the rush of the crowd. A circle formed round him too. Two old ladies, whom he had almost knocked down in his retreat, raised a great shrieking and outcry. The confusion was awful; all were asking questions, every one was shouting, every one was finding fault. The orchestra was silent. Our hero whirled round in his circle and mechanically, with a semblance of a smile, muttered something to himself, such as, "Why not?" and "that the polka, so far, at least, as he could see, was a new and very interesting dance, invented for the diversion of the ladies . . . but that since things had taken this turn, he was ready to consent." But Mr.

Golyadkin's consent no one apparently thought of asking. Our hero was suddenly aware that some one's hand was laid on his arm, that another hand was pressed against his back, that he was with peculiar solicitude being guided in a certain direction. At last he noticed that he was going straight to the door. Mr. Golyadkin wanted to say something, to do something. . . . But no, he no longer wanted to do anything. He only mechanically kept laughing in answer. At last he was aware that they were putting on his greatcoat, that his hat was thrust over his eyes; finally he felt that he was in the entry on the stairs in the dark and cold. At last he stumbled, he felt that he was falling down a precipice; he tried to cry out—and suddenly found himself in the courtyard. The air blew fresh on him, he stood still for a minute; at that very instant, the strains reached him of the orchestra striking up again. Mr. Golyadkin suddenly recalled it all; it seemed to him that all his flagging energies came back to him again. He had been standing as though riveted to the spot, but now he started off and rushed away headlong, anywhere, into the air, into freedom, wherever chance might take him.

CHAPTER V

IT was striking midnight from all the clock towers in Petersburg when Mr. Golyadkin, beside himself, ran out on the Fontanka Quay, close to the Ismailovsky Bridge, fleeing from his foes, from persecution, from a hailstorm of nips and pinches aimed at him, from the shrieks of excited old ladies, from the Ohs and Ahs of women and from the murderous eyes of Andrey Filippovitch. Mr. Golyadkin was killed—killed entirely, in the full sense of the word, and if he still preserved the power of running, it was simply through some sort of miracle, a miracle in which at last he refused himself to believe. It was an awful November night— wet, foggy, rainy, snowy, teeming with colds in the head, fevers, swollen faces, quinseys, inflammations of all kinds and descriptions—teeming, in fact, with all the gifts of a Petersburg November. The wind howled in the deserted streets, lifting up the black water of the canal above the rings on the bank, and irritably brushing against the lean lamp-posts which chimed in with its howling in a thin, shrill creak, keeping up the endless squeaky, jangling concert with which every inhabitant of Petersburg is so familiar. Snow and rain were falling both at once. Lashed by the wind, the streams of rainwater spurted almost horizontally, as though from a fireman's hose, pricking and stinging the face of the luckless Mr. Golyadkin like a thousand pins and needles. In the stillness of the night, broken only by the distant rumbling of carriages, the howl of the wind and the creaking of the lamp-posts, there was the dismal sound of the splash and gurgle of water, rushing from every roof, every porch, every pipe and every cornice, on to the granite of the pavement. There was not a soul, near or far, and, indeed, it seemed there could not be at such an hour and in such weather. And so only Mr. Golyadkin, alone with his despair, was fleeing in terror along the pavement of Fontanka, with his usual rapid little step, in haste to get home as soon as possible to his flat on the fourth storey in Shestilavotchny Street.

Though the snow, the rain, and all the nameless horrors of a raging snowstorm and fog, under a Petersburg November sky, were attacking Mr. Golyadkin, already shattered by misfortunes, were showing him no mercy, giving him no rest, drenching him to the bone, glueing up his eyelids, blowing right through him from all sides, baffling and perplexing him—though all this was hurled upon Mr. Golyadkin at once, as though conspiring and combining with all his enemies to make a grand day, evening, and night for him, in spite of all this Mr. Golyadkin was almost insensible to this final proof of the persecution of destiny: so violent had been the shock and the impression made upon him a few minutes before at the civil councillor Berendyev's! If any disinterested spectator could have glanced casually at Mr. Golyadkin's painful progress, he would instantly have grasped the awful horror of his pitiful plight and would certainly have said that Mr. Golyadkin looked as though he wanted to hide from himself, as though he were trying to run away from himself! Yes! It was really so. One may say more: Mr. Golyadkin did not want only to run away from himself, but to be obliterated, to cease to be, to return to dust. At the moment he took in nothing surrounding him, understood nothing of what was going on about him, and looked as though the miseries of the stormy night, of the long tramp, the rain, the snow, the wind, all the cruelty of the weather, did not exist for him. The golosh slipping off the boot on Mr. Golyadkin's right foot was left behind in the snow and slush on the pavement of Fontanka, and Mr. Golyadkin did not think of turning back to get it, did not, in fact, notice that he had lost it. He was so perplexed that, in spite of everything surrounding him, he stood several times stockstill in the middle of the pavement, completely possessed by the thought of his recent horrible humiliation; at that instant he was dying, disappearing; then he suddenly set off again like mad and ran and ran without looking back, as though he were pursued, as though he were fleeing from some still more awful calamity. . . . The position was truly awful! . . . At last Mr. Golyadkin halted in exhaustion, leaned on the railing in the attitude of a man whose nose has suddenly begun to bleed, and began looking intently at the black and troubled waters of the canal. There is no knowing what length of time he spent like this. All that is known is that at that instant Mr. Golyadkin reached such a pitch of despair, was so harassed, so tortured, so exhausted, and so weakened in what feeble faculties were left him that he forgot everything, forgot the Ismailovsky Bridge, forgot Shestilavotchny Street, forgot his present plight. . . . After all, what did it matter to him? The thing was done. The decision was affirmed and ratified; what could he do? All at once . . . all at once he started and involuntarily skipped a couple of paces aside. With unaccountable uneasiness he began gazing about him; but no one was there, nothing special had happened, and yet . . . and yet he fancied that just now, that very minute, some one was standing near him, beside him, also leaning on the railing, and—marvellous to relate!—had even said something to him, said something quickly, abruptly, not quite intelligibly, but something quite private, something concerning himself.

"Why, was it my fancy?" said Mr. Golyadkin, looking round once more. "But where am I standing? . . . Ech, ech," he thought finally, shaking his head, though he began gazing with an uneasy, miserable feeling into the damp, murky distance, straining his sight and doing his utmost to pierce with his shortsighted eyes the wet darkness that stretched all round him. There was nothing new, however, nothing special caught the eye of Mr. Golyadkin. Everything seemed to be all right, as it should be, that is, the snow was falling more violently, more thickly and in larger flakes, nothing could be seen twenty paces away, the lamp-posts creaked more shrilly than ever and the wind seemed to intone its melancholy song even more tearfully, more piteously, like an importunate beggar whining for a copper to get a crust of bread. At the same time a new sensation took possession of Mr. Golyadkin's whole being: agony upon agony, terror upon terror . . . a feverish tremor ran through his veins. The moment was insufferably unpleasant! "Well, it's no matter," he said, to encourage himself. "Well, no matter; perhaps it's no matter at all, and there's no stain on any one's honour. Perhaps it's as it should be," he went on, without understanding what he was saying. "Perhaps it will all be for the best in the end, and there will be nothing to complain of, and every one will be justified."

Talking like this and comforting himself with words, Mr. Golyadkin shook himself a little, shook off the snow which had drifted in thick layers on his hat, his collar, his overcoat, his tie, his boots and everything—

but his strange feeling, his strange, obscure misery he could not get rid of, could not shake off. Somewhere in the distance there was the boom of a cannon shot. "Ach, what weather!" thought our hero. "Tchoo! isn't there going to be a flood? It seems as though the water has risen so violently."

Mr. Golyadkin had hardly said or thought this when he saw a person coming towards him, belated, no doubt, like him, through some accident. An unimportant, casual incident, one might suppose, but for some unknown reason Mr. Golyadkin was troubled, even scared, and rather flurried. It was not that he was exactly afraid of some ill-intentioned man, but just that "perhaps . . . after all, who knows, this belated individual," flashed through Mr. Golyadkin's mind, "maybe he's that very thing, maybe he's the very principal thing in it, and isn't here for nothing, but is here with an object, crossing my path and provoking me." Possibly, however, he did not think this precisely, but only had a passing feeling of something like it—and very unpleasant. There was no time, however, for thinking and feeling. The stranger was already within two paces. Mr. Golyadkin, as he invariably did, hastened to assume a quite peculiar air, an air that expressed clearly that he, Golyadkin, kept himself to himself, that he was "all right," that the road was wide enough for all, and that he, Golyadkin, was not interfering with any one. Suddenly he stopped short as though petrified, as though struck by lightning, and quickly turned round after the figure which had only just passed him—turned as though some one had given him a tug from behind, as though the wind had turned him like a weathercock. The passer-by vanished quickly in the snowstorm. He, too, walked quickly; he was dressed like Mr. Golyadkin and, like him, too, wrapped up from head to foot, and he, too, tripped and trotted along the pavement of Fontanka with rapid little steps that suggested that he was a little scared.

"What—what is it?" whispered Mr. Golyadkin, smiling mistrustfully, though he trembled all over. An icy shiver ran down his back. Meanwhile, the stranger had vanished completely; there was no sound of his step, while Mr. Golyadkin still stood and gazed after him. At last, however, he gradually came to himself.

"Why, what's the meaning of it?" he thought with vexation. "Why, have I really gone out of my mind, or what?" He turned and went on his way, making his footsteps more rapid and frequent, and doing his best not to think of anything at all. He even closed his eyes at last with the same object. Suddenly, through the howling of the wind and the uproar of the storm, the sound of steps very close at hand reached his ears again. He started and opened his eyes. Again a rapidly approach-

ing figure stood out black before him, some twenty paces away. This little figure was hastening, tripping along, hurrying nervously; the distance between them grew rapidly less. Mr. Golyadkin could by now get
a full view of this second belated companion. He looked full at him and
cried out with amazement and horror; his legs gave way under him. It
was the same individual who had passed him ten minutes before, and
who now quite unexpectedly turned up facing him again. But this was
not the only marvel that struck Mr. Golyadkin. He was so amazed that
he stood still, cried out, tried to say something, and rushed to overtake
the stranger, even shouted something to him, probably anxious to stop
him as quickly as possible. The stranger did, in fact, stop ten paces from
Mr. Golyadkin, so that the light from the lamp-post that stood near fell
full upon his whole figure—stood still, turned to Mr. Golyadkin, and
with impatient and anxious face waited to hear what he would say.

"Excuse me, possibly I'm mistaken," our hero brought out in a qua-
vering voice.

The stranger in silence, and with an air of annoyance, turned and
rapidly went on his way, as though in haste to make up for the two seconds he had wasted on Mr. Golyadkin. As for the latter, he was quivering in every nerve, his knees shook and gave way under him, and with
a moan he squatted on a stone at the edge of the pavement. There really was reason, however, for his being so overwhelmed. The fact is that
this stranger seemed to him now somehow familiar. That would have
been nothing, though. But he recognized, almost certainly recognized
this man. He had often seen him, that man, had seen him some time,
and very lately too; where could it have been? Surely not yesterday?
But, again, that was not the chief thing that Mr. Golyadkin had often
seen him before; there was hardly anything special about the man; the
man at first sight would not have aroused any special attention. He was
just a man like any one else, a gentleman like all other gentlemen, of
course, and perhaps he had some good qualities and very valuable ones
too—in fact, he was a man who was quite himself. Mr. Golyadkin cher-
ished no sort of hatred or enmity, not even the slightest hostility towards
this man—quite the contrary, it would seem, indeed—and yet (and this
was the real point) he would not for any treasure on earth have been
willing to meet that man, and especially to meet him as he had done
now, for instance. We may say more: Mr. Golyadkin knew that man
perfectly well: he even knew what he was called, what his name was;
and yet nothing would have induced him, and again, for no treasure on
earth would he have consented to name him, to consent to acknowledge that he was called so-and-so, that his father's name was this and
his surname was that. Whether Mr. Golyadkin's stupefaction lasted a

short time or a long time, whether he was sitting for a long time on the stone of the pavement I cannot say; but, recovering himself a little at last, he suddenly fell to running, without looking round, as fast as his legs could carry him; his mind was preoccupied, twice he stumbled and almost fell—and through this circumstance his other boot was also bereaved of its golosh. At last Mr. Golyadkin slackened his pace a little to get breath, looked hurriedly round and saw that he had already, without being aware of it, run right across Fontanka, had crossed the Anitchkov Bridge, had passed part of the Nevsky Prospect and was now standing at the turning into Liteyny Street. Mr. Golyadkin turned into Liteyny Street. His position at that instant was like that of a man standing at the edge of a fearful precipice, while the earth is bursting open under him, is already shaking, moving, rocking for the last time, falling, drawing him into the abyss, and yet the luckless wretch has not the strength, nor the resolution, to leap back, to avert his eyes from the yawning gulf below; the abyss draws him and at last he leaps into it of himself, himself hastening the moment of his destruction. Mr. Golyadkin knew, felt and was firmly convinced that some other evil would certainly befall him on the way, that some unpleasantness would overtake him, that he would, for instance, meet his stranger once more: but—strange to say, he positively desired this meeting, considered it inevitable, and all he asked was that it might all be quickly over, that he should be relieved from his position in one way or another, but as soon as possible. And meanwhile he ran on and on, as though moved by some external force, for he felt a weakness and numbness in his whole being: he could not think of anything, though his thoughts caught at everything like brambles. A little lost dog, soaked and shivering, attached itself to Mr. Golyadkin, and ran beside him, scurrying along with tail and ears drooping, looking at him from time to time with timid comprehension. Some remote, long-forgotten idea—some memory of something that had happened long ago—came back into his mind now, kept knocking at his brain as with a hammer, vexing him and refusing to be shaken off.

"Ech, that horrid little cur!" whispered Mr. Golyadkin, not understanding himself.

At last he saw his stranger at the turning into Italyansky Street. But this time the stranger was not coming to meet him, but was going in the same direction as he was, and he, too, was running, a few steps in front. At last they turned into Shestilavotchny Street.

Mr. Golyadkin caught his breath. The stranger stopped exactly before the house in which Mr. Golyadkin lodged. He heard a ring at the bell and almost at the same time the grating of the iron bolt. The gate opened, the stranger stooped, darted in and disappeared. Almost at the same instant Mr. Golyadkin reached the spot and like an arrow flew in at the gate. Heedless of the grumbling porter, he ran, gasping for breath, into the yard, and immediately saw his interesting companion, whom he had lost sight of for a moment.

The stranger darted towards the staircase which led to Mr. Golyadkin's flat. Mr. Golyadkin rushed after him. The stairs were dark, damp and dirty. At every turning there were heaped-up masses of refuse from the flats, so that any unaccustomed stranger who found himself on the stairs in the dark was forced to travel to and fro for half an hour in danger of breaking his legs, cursing the stairs as well as the friends who lived in such an inconvenient place. But Mr. Golyadkin's companion seemed as though familiar with it, as though at home; he ran up lightly, without difficulty, showing a perfect knowledge of his surroundings. Mr. Golyadkin had almost caught him up; in fact, once or twice the stranger's coat flicked him on the nose. His heart stood still. The stranger stopped before the door of Mr. Golyadkin's flat, knocked on it, and (which would, however, have surprised Mr. Golyadkin at any other time) Petrushka, as though he had been sitting up in expectation, opened the door at once and, with a candle in his hand, followed the stranger as the latter went in. The hero of our story dashed into his lodging beside himself; without taking off his hat or coat he crossed the little passage and stood still in the doorway of his room, as though thunderstruck. All his presentiments had come true. All that he had dreaded and surmised was coming to pass in reality. His breath failed him, his head was in a whirl. The stranger, also in his coat and hat, was sitting before him on his bed, and with a faint smile, screwing up his eyes, nodded to him in a friendly way. Mr. Golyadkin wanted to scream, but could not—to protest in some way, but his strength failed him. His hair stood on end, and he almost fell down with horror. And, indeed, there was good reason. He recognized his nocturnal visitor. The nocturnal visitor was no other than himself—Mr. Golyadkin himself, another Mr. Golyadkin, but absolutely the same as himself—in fact, what is called a double in every respect. . . .

CHAPTER VI

At eight o'clock next morning Mr. Golyadkin woke up in his bed. At once all the extraordinary incidents of the previous day and the wild, incredible night, with all its almost impossible adventures, presented themselves to his imagination and memory with terrifying vividness. Such intense, diabolical malice on the part of his enemies, and, above all, the final proof of that malice, froze Mr. Golyadkin's heart. But at the same time it was all so strange, incomprehensible, wild, it seemed so impossible, that it was really hard to credit himself that it was all an incredible delusion, a passing aberration of the fancy, a darkening of the mind, if he had not fortunately known by bitter experience to what lengths spite will sometimes carry any one, what a pitch of ferocity an enemy may reach when he is bent on revenging his honour and prestige. Besides, Mr. Golyadkin's exhausted limbs, his heavy head, his aching back, and the malignant cold in his head bore vivid witness to the probability of his expedition of the previous night and upheld the reality of it, and to some extent of all that had happened during that expedition. And, indeed, Mr. Golyadkin had known long, long before that something was being got up among them, that there was some one else with them. But after all, thinking it over thoroughly, he made up his mind to keep quiet, to submit and not to protest for the time.

"They are simply plotting to frighten me, perhaps, and when they see that I don't mind, that I make no protest, but keep perfectly quiet and put up with it meekly, they'll give it up, they'll give it up of themselves, give it up of their own accord."

Such, then, were the thoughts in the mind of Mr. Golyadkin as, stretching in his bed, trying to rest his exhausted limbs, he waited for Petrushka to come into his room as usual. . . . He waited for a full quarter of an hour. He heard the lazy scamp fiddling about with the samovar behind the screen, and yet he could not bring himself to call him. We may say more: Mr. Golyadkin was a little afraid of confronting Petrushka.

"Why, goodness knows," he thought, "goodness knows how that rascal looks at it all. He keeps on saying nothing, but he has his own ideas."

At last the door creaked and Petrushka came in with a tray in his hands. Mr. Golyadkin stole a timid glance at him, impatiently waiting to see what would happen, waiting to see whether he would not say something about a certain circumstance. But Petrushka said nothing; he was, on the contrary, more silent, more glum and ill-humoured than usual; he looked askance from under his brows at everything; altogether it was evident that he was very much put out about something; he did not even once glance at his master, which, by the way, rather piqued the latter. Setting all he had brought on the table, he turned and went out of the room without a word.

"He knows, he knows, he knows all about it, the scoundrel!" Mr.

Golyadkin grumbled to himself as he took his tea. Yet our hero did not address a single question to his servant, though Petrushka came into his room several times afterwards on various errands. Mr. Golyadkin was in great trepidation of spirit. He dreaded going to the office. He had a strong presentiment that there he would find something that would not be "just so."

"You may be sure," he thought, "that as soon as you go you will light upon something! Isn't it better to endure in patience? Isn't it better to wait a bit now? Let them do what they like there; but I'd better stay here a bit to-day, recover my strength, get better, and think over the whole affair more thoroughly, then afterwards I could seize the right moment, fall upon them like snow from the sky, and get off scot free myself."

Reasoning like this, Mr. Golyadkin smoked pipe after pipe; time was flying. It was already nearly half-past nine.

"Why, it's half-past nine already," thought Mr. Golyadkin; "it's late for me to make my appearance. Besides, I'm ill, of course I'm ill, I'm certainly ill; who denies it? What's the matter with me? If they send to make inquiries, let the executive clerk come; and, indeed, what is the matter with me really? My back aches, I have a cough, and a cold in my head; and, in fact, it's out of the question for me to go out, utterly out of the question in such weather. I might be taken ill and, very likely, die; nowadays especially the death-rate is so high. . . ."

With such reasoning Mr. Golyadkin succeeded at last in setting his conscience at rest, and defended himself against the reprimands he expected from Andrey Filippovitch for neglect of his duty. As a rule in such cases our hero was particularly fond of justifying himself in his own eyes with all sorts of irrefutable arguments, and so completely setting his conscience at rest. And so now, having completely soothed his conscience, he took up his pipe, filled it, and had no sooner settled down comfortably to smoke, when he jumped up quickly from the sofa, flung away the pipe, briskly washed, shaved, and brushed his hair, got into his uniform and so on, snatched up some papers, and flew off to the office.

Mr. Golyadkin went into his department timidly, in quivering expectation of something unpleasant—an expectation which was none the less disagreeable for being vague and unconscious; he sat timidly down in his invariable place next the head clerk, Anton Antonovitch Syetotchkin. Without looking at anything or allowing his attention to be distracted, he plunged into the contents of the papers that lay before him. He made up his mind and vowed to himself to avoid, as far as possible, anything provocative, anything that might compromise him, such as indiscreet questions, jests, or unseemly allusions to any incidents of the previous evening; he made up his mind also to abstain from the usual interchange of civilities with his colleagues, such as inquiries after health and such like. But evidently it was impossible, out of the question, to keep to this. Anxiety and uneasiness in regard to anything near him that was annoying always worried him far more than the annoyance itself. And that was why, in spite of his inward vows to refrain from entering into anything, whatever happened, and to keep aloof from everything, Mr. Golyadkin from time to time, on the sly, very, very quietly, raised his head and stealthily looked about him to right and to left, peeped at the countenances of his colleagues, and tried to gather whether there were not something new and particular in them referring to himself and with sinister motives concealed from him. He assumed that there must be a connection between all that had happened yesterday and all that surrounded him now. At last, in his misery, he began to long for something—goodness knows what—to happen to put an end to it—even some calamity—he did not care. At this point destiny caught Mr. Golyadkin: he had hardly felt this desire when his doubts were solved in the strangest and most unexpected manner.

The door leading from the next room suddenly gave a soft and timid creak, as though to indicate that the person about to enter was a very unimportant one, and a figure, very familiar to Mr. Golyadkin, stood shyly before the very table at which our hero was seated. The latter did not raise his head—no, he only stole a glance at him, the tiniest glance; but he knew all, he understood all, to every detail. He grew hot with shame, and buried his devoted head in his papers with precisely the same object with which the ostrich, pursued by hunters, hides his head in the burning sand. The new arrival bowed to Andrey Filippovitch, and thereupon he heard a voice speaking in the regulation tone of condescending politeness with which all persons in authority address their subordinates in public offices.

"Take a seat here," said Andrey Filippovitch, motioning the newcomer to Anton Antonovitch's table. "Here, opposite Mr. Golyadkin, and we'll soon give you something to do."

Andrey Filippovitch ended by making a rapid gesture that decorously admonished the newcomer of his duty, and then he immediately became engrossed in the study of the papers that lay in a heap before him.

Mr. Golyadkin lifted his eyes at last, and that he did not fall into a swoon was simply because he had foreseen it all from the first, that he had been forewarned from the first, guessing in his soul who the stranger was. Mr. Golyadkin's first movement was to look quickly about him, to see whether there were any whispering, any office joke being cracked on the subject, whether any one's face was agape with wonder, whether, indeed, some one had not fallen under the table from terror. But to his intense astonishment there was no sign of anything of the sort. The behaviour of his colleagues and companions surprised him. It seemed contrary to the dictates of common sense. Mr. Golyadkin was positively scared at this extraordinary reticence. The fact spoke for itself; it was a strange, horrible, uncanny thing. It was enough to rouse any one. All this, of course, only passed rapidly through Mr. Golyadkin's mind. He felt as though he were burning in a slow fire. And, indeed, there was enough to make him. The figure that was sitting opposite Mr. Golyadkin now was his terror, was his shame, was his nightmare of the evening before; in short, was Mr. Golyadkin himself, not the Mr. Golyadkin who was sitting now in his chair with his mouth wide open and his pen petrified in his hand, not the one who acted as assistant to his chief, not the one who liked to efface himself and slink away in the crowd, not the one whose deportment plainly said, "Don't touch me and I won't touch you," or, "Don't interfere with me, you see I'm not touching you"; no, this was another Mr. Golyadkin, quite different, yet, at the same time, exactly like the first—the same height, the same figure, the same clothes, the same baldness; in fact, nothing, absolutely nothing, was lacking to complete the likeness, so that if one were to set them side by side, nobody, absolutely nobody, could have undertaken to distinguish which was the real Golyadkin and which was the counterfeit, which was the old one and which was the new one, which was the original and which was the copy.

Our hero was—if the comparison can be made—in the position of a man upon whom some practical joker has stealthily, by way of jest, turned a burning-glass.

"What does it mean? Is it a dream?" he wondered. "Is it reality or the continuation of what happened yesterday? And besides, by what right is this all being done? Who sanctioned such a clerk, who authorized this? Am I asleep, am I in a waking dream?"

Mr. Golyadkin tried pinching himself, even tried to screw up his courage to pinch some one else. . . . No, it was not a dream, and that was all about it. Mr. Golyadkin felt that the sweat was trickling down him in big drops; he felt that what was happening to him was something incredible, unheard of, and for that very reason was, to complete his misery, utterly unseemly, for Mr. Golyadkin realized and felt how disadvantageous it was to be the first example of such a burlesque adventure. He even began to doubt his own existence, and though he was prepared for anything and had been longing for his doubts to be settled in any way whatever, yet the actual reality was startling in its unexpectedness. His misery was poignant and overwhelming. At times he lost all power of thought and memory. Coming to himself after such a moment, he noticed that he was mechanically and unconsciously moving the pen over the paper. Mistrustful of himself, he began going over what he had written—and could make nothing of it. At last the other Mr. Golyadkin, who had been sitting discreetly and decorously at the table, got up and disappeared through the door into the other room. Mr. Golyadkin looked round—everything was quiet; he heard nothing but the scratching of pens, the rustle of turning over pages, and conversation in the corners furthest from Andrey Filippovitch's seat. Mr. Golyadkin looked at Anton Antonovitch, and as, in all probability, our hero's countenance fully reflected his real condition and harmonized with the whole position, and was consequently, from one point of view, very remarkable, good-natured Anton Antonovitch, laying aside his pen, inquired after his health with marked sympathy.

"I'm very well, thank God, Anton Antonovitch," said Mr. Golyadkin, stammering. "I am perfectly well, Anton Antonovitch. I am all right now, Anton Antonovitch," he added uncertainly, not yet fully trusting Anton Antonovitch, whose name he had mentioned so often.

"I fancied you were not quite well: though that's not to be wondered at; no, indeed! Nowadays especially there's such a lot of illness going about. Do you know . . ."

"Yes, Anton Antonovitch, I know there is such a lot of illness . . . I did not mean that, Anton Antonovitch," Mr. Golyadkin went on, looking intently at Anton Antonovitch. "You see, Anton Antonovitch, I don't even know how you, that is, I mean to say, how to approach this matter, Anton Antonovitch. . . ."

"How so? I really . . . do you know . . . I must confess I don't quite understand; you must . . . you must explain, you know, in what way you are in difficulties," said Anton Antonovitch, beginning to be in difficulties himself, seeing that there were actually tears in Mr. Golyadkin's eyes.

"Really, Anton Antonovitch . . . I . . . here . . . there's a clerk here, Anton Antonovitch . . ."

"Well! I don't understand now."

"I mean to say, Anton Antonovitch, there's a new clerk here."

"Yes, there is; a namesake of yours."

"What?" cried Mr. Golyadkin.

"I say a namesake of yours; his name's Golyadkin too. Isn't he a brother of yours?"

"No, Anton Antonovitch, I . . ."

"H'm! you don't say so! Why, I thought he must be a relation of yours. Do you know, there's a sort of family likeness."

Mr. Golyadkin was petrified with astonishment, and for the moment he could not speak. To treat so lightly such a horrible, unheard-of thing, a thing undeniably rare and curious in its way, a thing which would have amazed even an unconcerned spectator, to talk of a family resemblance when he could see himself as in a looking-glass!

"Do you know, Yakov Petrovitch, what I advise you to do?" Anton Antonovitch went on. "Go and consult a doctor. Do you know, you look somehow quite unwell. Your eyes look peculiar . . . you know, there's a peculiar expression in them."

"No, Anton Antonovitch, I feel, of course . . . that is, I keep wanting to ask about this clerk."

"Well?"

"That is, have not you noticed, Anton Antonovitch, something peculiar about him, something very marked?"

"That is . . . ?"

"That is, I mean, Anton Antonovitch, a striking likeness with somebody, for instance; with me, for instance? You spoke just now, you see, Anton Antonovitch, of a family likeness. You let slip the remark. . . . You know there really are sometimes twins exactly alike, like two drops of water, so that they can't be told apart. Well, it's that that I mean."

"To be sure," said Anton Antonovitch, after a moment's thought, speaking as though he were struck by the fact for the first time; "yes, indeed! You are right, there is a striking likeness, and you are quite right in what you say. You really might be mistaken for one another," he went on, opening his eyes wider and wider; "and, do you know, Yakov Petrovitch, it's positively a marvellous likeness, fantastic, in fact, as the saying is; that is, just as you . . . Have you observed, Yakov Petrovitch? I wanted to ask you to explain it; yes, I must confess I didn't take particular notice at first. It's wonderful, it's really wonderful! And, you know, you are not a native of these parts, are you, Yakov Petrovitch?"

"No."

"He is not from these parts, you know, either. Perhaps he comes from the same part of the country as you do. Where, may I make bold to inquire, did your mother live for the most part?"

"You said . . . you say, Anton Antonovitch, that he is not a native of these parts?"

"No, he is not. And, indeed, how strange it is!" continued the talkative Anton Antonovitch, for whom it was a genuine treat to gossip. "It may well arouse curiosity; and yet, you know, you might often pass him by, brush against him, without noticing anything. But you mustn't be upset about it. It's a thing that does happen. Do you know, the same thing, I must tell you, happened to my aunt on my mother's side; she saw her own double before her death . . ."

"No, I—excuse my interrupting you, Anton Antonovitch—I wanted to find out, Anton Antonovitch, how that clerk . . . that is, on what footing is he here?"

"In place of Semyon Ivanovitch, to fill the vacancy left by his death; the post was vacant, so he was appointed. Do you know, I'm told poor dear Semyon Ivanovitch left three children, all tiny dots. The widow fell at the feet of his Excellency. They do say she's hiding something; she's got a bit of money, but she's hiding it."

"No, Anton Antonovitch, I was still referring to that circumstance."

"You mean . . . ? To be sure! but why are you so interested in that? I tell you not to upset yourself. All this is temporary to some extent. Why, after all, you know, you have nothing to do with it. So it has been ordained by God Almighty, it's His will, and it is sinful repining. His wisdom is apparent in it. And as far as I can make out, Yakov Petrovitch, you are not to blame in any way. There are all sorts of strange things in the world! Mother Nature is liberal with her gifts, and you are not called upon to answer for it, you won't be responsible. Here, for instance, you have heard, I expect, of those—what's their name?—oh, the Siamese twins who are joined together at the back, live and eat and sleep together. I'm told they get a lot of money."

"Allow me, Anton Antonovitch . . ."

"I understand, I understand! Yes! But what of it? It's no matter, I tell you, as far as I can see there's nothing for you to upset yourself about. After all, he's a clerk—as a clerk he seems to be a capable man. He says his name is Golyadkin, that he's not a native of this district, and that he's a titular councillor. He had a personal interview with his Excellency."

"And how did his Excellency . . . ?"

"It was all right; I am told he gave a satisfactory account of himself, gave his reasons, said, 'It's like this, your Excellency,' and that he was without means and anxious to enter the service, and would be particularly flattered to be serving under his Excellency . . . all that was proper, you know; he expressed himself neatly. He must be a sensible man. But of course he came with a recommendation; he couldn't have got in without that. . . ."

"Oh, from whom . . . that is, I mean, who is it has had a hand in this shameful business?"

"Yes, a good recommendation, I'm told; his Excellency, I'm told, laughed with Andrey Filippovitch."

"Laughed with Andrey Filippovitch?"

"Yes, he only just smiled and said that it was all right, and that he had nothing against it, so long as he did his duty. . . ."

"Well, and what more? You relieve me to some extent, Anton Antonovitch; go on, I entreat you."

"Excuse me, I must tell you again. . . . Well, then, come, it's nothing, it's a very simple matter; you mustn't upset yourself, I tell you, and there's nothing suspicious about it. . . ."

"No. I . . . that is, Anton Antonovitch, I want to ask you, didn't his Excellency say anything more . . . about me, for instance?"

"Well! To be sure! No, nothing of the sort; you can set your mind quite at rest. You know it is, of course, a rather striking circumstance, and at first . . . why, here, I, for instance, I scarcely noticed it. I really don't know why I didn't notice it till you mentioned it. But you can set your mind at rest entirely. He said nothing particular, absolutely nothing," added good-natured Anton Antonovitch, getting up from his chair.

"So then, Anton Antonovitch, I . . ."

"Oh, you must excuse me. Here I've been gossiping about these trivial matters, and I've business that is important and urgent. I must inquire about it."

"Anton Antonovitch!" Andrey Filippovitch's voice sounded, summoning him politely, "his Excellency has been asking for you."

"This minute, I'm coming this minute, Andrey Filippovitch." And Anton Antonovitch, taking a pile of papers, flew off first to Andrey Filippovitch and then into his Excellency's room.

"Then what is the meaning of it?" thought Mr. Golyadkin. "Is there some sort of game going on? So the wind's in that quarter now. . . . That's just as well; so things have taken a much pleasanter turn," our hero said to himself, rubbing his hands, and so delighted that he scarcely knew where he was. "So our position is an ordinary thing. So it turns out to be all nonsense, it comes to nothing at all. No one has done anything really, and they are not budging, the rascals, they are sitting busy over their work; that's splendid, splendid! I like the good-natured fellow, I've always liked him, and I'm always ready to respect him . . . though

it must be said one doesn't know what to think; this Anton Antonovitch
... I'm afraid to trust him; his hair's very grey, and he's so old he's getting shaky. It's an immense and glorious thing that his Excellency said
nothing, and let it pass! It's a good thing! I approve! Only why does
Andrey Filippovitch interfere with his grins? What's he got to do with
it? The old rogue. Always on my track, always, like a black cat, on the
watch to run across a man's path, always thwarting and annoying a man,
always annoying and thwarting a man. . . ."

Mr. Golyadkin looked around him again, and again his hopes
revived. Yet he felt that he was troubled by one remote idea, an unpleasant idea. It even occurred to him that he might try somehow to make
up to the clerks, to be the first in the field even (perhaps when leaving
the office or going up to them as though about his work), to drop a hint
in the course of conversation, saying, "This is how it is, what a striking
likeness, gentlemen, a strange circumstance, a burlesque farce!"—that
is, treat it all lightly, and in this way sound the depth of the danger.
"Devils breed in still waters," our hero concluded inwardly.

Mr. Golyadkin, however, only contemplated this; he thought better
of it in time. He realized that this would be going too far. "That's your
temperament," he said to himself, tapping himself lightly on the forehead; "as soon as you gain anything you are delighted! You're a simple
soul! No, you and I had better be patient, Yakov Petrovitch; let us wait
and be patient!"

Nevertheless, as we have mentioned already, Mr. Golyadkin was
buoyed up with the most confident hopes, feeling as though he had
risen from the dead.

"No matter," he thought, "it's as though a hundred tons had been lifted off my chest! Here is a circumstance, to be sure! The box has been
opened by lifting the lid. Krylov is right, a clever chap, a rogue, that
Krylov, and a great fable-writer! And as for him, let him work in the
office, and good luck to him so long as he doesn't meddle or interfere
with anyone; let him work in the office—I consent and approve!"

Meanwhile the hours were passing, flying by, and before he noticed
the time it struck four. The office was closed. Andrey Filippovitch took
his hat, and all followed his example in due course. Mr. Golyadkin daw-
dled a little on purpose, long enough to be the last to go out when all
the others had gone their several ways. Going out from the street he felt
as though he were in Paradise, so that he even felt inclined to go a
longer way round, and to walk along the Nevsky Prospect.

"To be sure this is destiny," thought our hero, "this unexpected turn
in affairs. And the weather's more cheerful, and the frost and the little
sledges. And the frost suits the Russian, the Russian gets on capitally

with the frost. I like the Russian. And the dear little snow, and the first few flakes in autumn; the sportsman would say, 'It would be nice to go shooting hares in the first snow.' Well, there, it doesn't matter."

This was how Mr. Golyadkin's enthusiasm found expression. Yet something was fretting in his brain, not exactly melancholy, but at times he had such a gnawing at his heart that he did not know how to find relief.

"Let us wait for the day, though, and then we shall rejoice. And, after all, you know, what does it matter? Come, let us think it over, let us look at it. Come, let us consider it, my young friend, let us consider it. Why, a man's exactly like you in the first place, absolutely the same. Well, what is there in that? If there is such a man, why should I weep over it? What is it to me? I stand aside, I whistle to myself, and that's all! That's what I laid myself open to, and that's all about it! Let him work in the office! Well, it's strange and marvellous, they say, that the Siamese twins . . . But why bring in the Siamese twins? They are twins, of course, but even great men, you know, sometimes look queer creatures. In fact, we know from history that the famous Suvorov used to crow like a cock. . . . But there, he did all that with political motives; and he was a great general . . . but what are generals, after all? But I keep myself to myself, that's all, and I don't care about any one else, and, secure in my innocence, I scorn my enemies. I am not one to intrigue, and I'm proud of it. Genuine, straightforward, neat and nice, meek and mild."

All at once Mr. Golyadkin broke off, his tongue failed him and he began trembling like a leaf; he even closed his eyes for a minute. Hoping, however, that the object of his terror was only an illusion, he opened his eyes at last and stole a timid glance to the right. No, it was not an illusion! . . . His acquaintance of that morning was tripping along by his side, smiling, peeping into his face, and apparently seeking an opportunity to begin a conversation with him. The conversation was not begun, however. They both walked like this for about fifty paces. All Mr. Golyadkin's efforts were concentrated on muffling himself up, hiding himself in his coat and pulling his hat down as far as possible over his eyes. To complete his mortification, his companion's coat and hat looked as though they had been taken off Mr. Golyadkin himself.

"Sir," our hero articulated at last, trying to speak almost in a whisper, and not looking at his companion, "we are going different ways, I believe. . . . I am convinced of it, in fact," he said, after a brief pause. "I am convinced, indeed, that you quite understand me," he added, rather severely, in conclusion.

"I could have wished . . ." his companion pronounced at last, "I

could have wished . . . no doubt you will be magnanimous and pardon
me . . . I don't know to whom to address myself here . . . my circumstances . . . I trust you will pardon my intrusiveness. I fancied, indeed,
that, moved by compassion, you showed some interest in me this morning. On my side, I felt drawn to you from the first moment. I . . ."

At this point Mr. Golyadkin inwardly wished that his companion
might sink into the earth.

"If I might venture to hope that you would accord me an indulgent
hearing, Yakov Petrovitch . . ."

"We—here, we—we . . . you had better come home with me,"
answered Mr. Golyadkin. "We will cross now to the other side of the
Nevsky Prospect, it will be more convenient for us there, and then by
the little back street . . . we'd better go by the back street."

"Very well, by all means let us go by the back street," our hero's meek
companion responded timidly, suggesting by the tone of his reply that
it was not for him to choose, and that in his position he was quite prepared to accept the back street. As for Mr. Golyadkin, he was utterly
unable to grasp what was happening to him. He could not believe in
himself. He could not get over his amazement.

CHAPTER VII

HE recovered himself a little on the staircase as he went up to his flat.

"Oh, I'm a sheep's head," he railed at himself inwardly. "Where am
I taking him? I am thrusting my head into the noose. What will
Petrushka think, seeing us together? What will the scoundrel dare to
imagine now? He's suspicious. . . ."

But it was too late to regret it. Mr. Golyadkin knocked at the door; it
was opened, and Petrushka began taking off the visitor's coat as well as
his master's. Mr. Golyadkin looked askance, just stealing a glance at
Petrushka, trying to read his countenance and divine what he was thinking. But to his intense astonishment he saw that his servant showed no
trace of surprise, but seemed, on the contrary, to be expecting something of the sort. Of course he did look morose, as it was; he kept his
eyes turned away and looked as though he would like to fall upon somebody.

"Hasn't somebody bewitched them all to-day?" thought our hero.
"Some devil must have got round them. There certainly must be some-

thing peculiar in the whole lot of them to-day. Damn it all, what a worry it is!"

Such were Mr. Golyadkin's thoughts and reflections as he led his visitor into his room and politely asked him to sit down. The visitor appeared to be greatly embarrassed, he was very shy, and humbly watched every movement his host made, caught his glance, and seemed trying to divine his thoughts from them. There was a down-trodden, crushed, scared look about all his gestures, so that—if the comparison may be allowed—he was at that moment rather like the man who, having lost his clothes, is dressed up in somebody else's: the sleeves work up to the elbows, the waist is almost up to his neck, and he keeps every minute pulling down the short waistcoat; he wriggles sideways and turns away, tries to hide himself, or peeps into every face, and listens whether people are talking of his position, laughing at him or putting him to shame—and he is crimson with shame and over-whelmed with confusion and wounded vanity. . . . Mr. Golyadkin put down his hat in the window, and carelessly sent it flying to the floor. The visitor darted at once to pick it up, brushed off the dust, and carefully put it back, while he laid his own on the floor near a chair, on the edge of which he meekly seated himself. This little circumstance did something to open Mr. Golyadkin's eyes; he realized that the man was in great straits, and so did not put himself out for his visitor as he had done at first, very properly leaving all that to the man himself. The visitor, for his part, did nothing either; whether he was shy, a little ashamed, or from politeness was waiting for his host to begin is not certain and would be difficult to determine. At that moment Petrushka came in; he stood still in the doorway, and fixed his eyes in the direction furthest from where the visitor and his master were seated.

"Shall I bring in dinner for two?" he said carelessly, in a husky voice.

"I—I don't know . . . you . . . yes, bring dinner for two, my boy."

Petrushka went out. Mr. Golyadkin glanced at his visitor. The latter crimsoned to his ears. Mr. Golyadkin was a kindhearted man, and so in the kindness of his heart he at once elaborated a theory.

"The fellow's hard up," he thought. "Yes, and in his situation only one day. Most likely he's suffered in his time. Maybe his good clothes are all that he has, and nothing to get him a dinner. Ah, poor fellow, how crushed he seems! But no matter; in a way it's better so. . . . Excuse me," began Mr. Golyadkin, "allow me to ask what I may call you."

"I . . . I . . . I'm Yakov Petrovitch," his visitor almost whispered, as though conscience-stricken and ashamed, as though apologizing for being called Yakov Petrovitch too.

"Yakov Petrovitch!" repeated our hero, unable to conceal his confusion.

"Yes, just so. . . . The same name as yours," responded the meek visitor, venturing to smile and speak a little jocosely. But at once he drew back, assuming a very serious air, though a little disconcerted, noticing that his host was in no joking mood.

"You . . . allow me to ask you, to what am I indebted for the honour . . . ?"

"Knowing your generosity and your benevolence," interposed the visitor in a rapid but timid voice, half rising from his seat, "I have ventured to appeal to you and to beg for your . . . acquaintance and protection . . ." he concluded, choosing his phrases with difficulty and trying to select words not too flattering or servile, that he might not compromise his dignity and not so bold as to suggest an unseemly equality. In fact, one may say the visitor behaved like a gentlemanly beggar with a darned waistcoat, with an honourable passport in his pocket, who has not yet learnt by practice to hold out his hand properly for alms.

"You perplex me," answered Mr. Golyadkin, gazing round at himself, his walls and his visitor. "In what could I . . . that is, I mean, in what way could I be of service to you?"

"I felt drawn to you, Yakov Petrovitch, at first sight, and, graciously forgive me, I built my hopes on you—I made bold to build my hopes on you, Yakov Petrovitch. I . . . I'm in a desperate plight here, Yakov Petrovitch; I'm poor, I've had a great deal of trouble, Yakov Petrovitch, and have only recently come here. Learning that you, with your innate goodness and excellence of heart, are of the same name . . ."

Mr. Golyadkin frowned.

"Of the same name as myself and a native of the same district, I made up my mind to appeal to you, and to make known to you my difficult position."

"Very good, very good; I really don't know what to say," Mr. Golyadkin responded in an embarrassed voice. "We'll have a talk after dinner. . . ."

The visitor bowed; dinner was brought in. Petrushka laid the table, and Mr. Golyadkin and his visitor proceeded to partake of it. The dinner did not last long, for they were both in a hurry, the host because he felt ill at ease, and was, besides, ashamed that the dinner was a poor one—he was partly ashamed because he wanted to give the visitor a good meal, and partly because he wanted to show him he did not live like a beggar. The visitor, on his side too, was in terrible confusion and extremely embarrassed. When he had finished the piece of bread he had taken, he was afraid to put out his hand to take another piece, was ashamed to help himself to the best morsels, and was continually assuring his host that he was not at all hungry, that the dinner was excellent, that he was absolutely satisfied with it, and should not forget it to his dying day. When the meal was over Mr. Golyadkin lighted his pipe, and offered a second, which was brought in, to the visitor. They sat facing each other, and the visitor began telling his adventures.

Mr. Golyadkin junior's story lasted for three or four hours. His history was, however, composed of the most trivial and wretched, if one may say so, incidents. It dealt with details of service in some lawcourt in the provinces, of prosecutors and presidents, of some department intrigues, of the depravity of some registration clerks, of an inspector, of the sudden appointment of a new chief in the department, of how the second Mr. Golyadkin had suffered, quite without any fault on his part; of his aged aunt, Pelagea Semyonovna; of how, through various intrigues on the part of his enemies, he had lost his situation, and had come to Petersburg on foot; of the harassing and wretched time he had spent here in Petersburg, how for a long time he had tried in vain to get a job, had spent all his money, had nothing left, had been living almost in the street, lived on a crust of bread and washed it down with his tears, slept on the bare floor, and finally how some good Christian had exerted himself on his behalf, had given him an introduction, and had nobly got him into a new berth. Mr. Golyadkin's visitor shed tears as he told his story, and wiped his eyes with a blue-check handkerchief that looked like oilcloth. He ended by making a clean breast of it to Mr. Golyadkin, and confessing that he was not only for the time without means of subsistence and money for a decent lodging, but had not even the wherewithal to fit himself out properly, so that he had not, he said in conclusion, been able to get together enough for a pair of wretched boots, and that he had had to hire a uniform for the time.

Mr. Golyadkin was melted; he was genuinely touched. Even though his visitor's story was the paltriest story, every word of it was like heavenly manna to his heart. The fact was that Mr. Golyadkin was beginning to forget his last misgivings, to surrender his soul to freedom and rejoicing, and at last mentally dubbed himself a fool. It was all so natural! And what a thing to break his heart over, what a thing to be so distressed about! To be sure there was, there really was, one ticklish circumstance—but, after all, it was not a misfortune; it could be no disgrace to a man, it could not cast a slur on his honour or ruin his career, if he were innocent, since nature herself was mixed up in it. Moreover, the visitor begged for protection, wept, railed at destiny, seemed such an artless, pitiful, insignificant person, with no craft or malice about him, and he seemed now to be ashamed himself, though perhaps on different grounds, of the strange resemblance of his countenance with that of Mr. Golyadkin's. His behaviour was absolutely unimpeachable; his one desire was to please his host, and he looked as a man looks who feels conscience-stricken and to blame in regard to some one else. If any doubtful point were touched upon, for instance, the visitor at once agreed with Mr. Golyadkin's opinion. If by mistake he advanced an opinion in opposition to Mr. Golyadkin's, and afterwards noticed that he had made a slip, he immediately corrected his mistake, explained himself and made it clear that he meant the same thing as his host, that he thought as he did and took the same view of everything as he did. In fact, the visitor made every possible effort to "make up to" Mr. Golyadkin, so that the latter made up his mind at last that his visitor must be a very amiable person in every way. Meanwhile, tea was brought in; it was nearly nine o'clock. Mr. Golyadkin felt in a very good-humour, grew lively and skittish, let himself go a little, and finally plunged into a most animated and interesting conversation with his visitor. In his festive moments Mr. Golyadkin was fond of telling interesting anecdotes. So now he told the visitor a great deal about Petersburg, about its entertainments and attractions, about the theatre, the clubs, about Brülov's picture, and about the two Englishmen who came from England to Petersburg on purpose to look at the iron railing of the Summer Garden, and returned at once when they had seen it; about the office; about Olsufy Ivanovitch and Andrey Filippovitch; about the way that Russia was progressing, was hour by hour progressing towards a state of perfection, so that

"Art and letters flourish here to-day";

about an anecdote he had lately read in the *Northern Bee* concerning a boa-constrictor in India of immense strength; about Baron Brambeus, and so on. In short, Mr. Golyadkin was quite happy, first, because his mind was at rest, secondly, because, so far from being afraid of his enemies, he was quite prepared now to challenge them all to mortal combat; thirdly, because he was now in the rôle of patron and was doing a good deed. Yet he was conscious at the bottom of his heart that he was not perfectly happy, that there was still a hidden worm gnawing at his heart, though it was only a tiny one. He was extremely worried by the thought of the previous evening at Olsufy Ivanovitch's. He would have given a great deal now for nothing to have happened of what took place then.

"It's no matter, though!" our hero decided at last, and he firmly resolved in his heart to behave well in future and never to be guilty of such pranks again. As Mr. Golyadkin was now completely worked up, and had suddenly become almost blissful, the fancy took him to have a jovial time. Rum was brought in by Petrushka, and punch was prepared. The visitor and his host drained a glass each, and then a second. The visitor appeared even more amiable than before, and gave more than one proof of his frankness and charming character; he entered keenly into Mr. Golyadkin's joy, seemed only to rejoice in his rejoicing, and to look upon him as his one and only benefactor. Taking up a pen and a sheet of paper, he asked Mr. Golyadkin not to look at what he was going to write, but afterwards showed his host what he had written. It turned out to be a verse of four lines, written with a good deal of feeling, in excellent language and handwriting, and evidently was the composition of the amiable visitor himself. The lines were as follows—

> "If thou forget me,
> I shall not forget thee;
> Though all things may be,
> Do not thou forget me."

With tears in his eyes Mr. Golyadkin embraced his companion, and, completely overcome by his feelings, he began to initiate his friend into some of his own secrets and private affairs, Andrey Filippovitch and Klara Olsufyevna being prominent in his remarks.

"Well, you may be sure we shall get on together, Yakov Petrovitch," said our hero to his visitor. "You and I will take to each other like fish to the water, Yakov Petrovitch; we shall be like brothers; we'll be cunning, my dear fellow, we'll work together; we'll get up an intrigue, too, to pay them out. To pay them out we'll get up an intrigue too. And don't you trust any of them. I know you, Yakov Petrovitch, and I understand your character; you'll tell them everything straight out, you know, you're a guileless soul! You must hold aloof from them all, my boy."

His companion entirely agreed with him, thanked Mr. Golyadkin, and he, too, grew tearful at last.

"Do you know, Yasha," Mr. Golyadkin went on in a shaking voice, weak with emotion, "you must stay with me for a time, or stay with me for ever. We shall get on together. What do you say, brother, eh? And don't you worry or repine because there's such a strange circumstance about us now; it's a sin to repine, brother; it's nature! And Mother Nature is liberal with her gifts, so there, brother Yasha! It's from love for you that I speak, from brotherly love. But we'll be cunning, Yasha; we'll lay a mine, too, and we'll make them laugh the other side of their mouths."

They reached their third and fourth glasses of punch at last, and then Mr. Golyadkin began to be aware of two sensations: the one that he was extraordinarily happy, and the other that he could not stand upon his legs. The guest was, of course, invited to stay the night. A bed was somehow made up on two chairs. Mr. Golyadkin junior declared that under a friend's roof the bare floor would be a soft bed, that for his part he could sleep anywhere, humbly and gratefully; that he was in paradise now, that he had been through a great deal of trouble and grief in his time; he had seen ups and downs, had all sorts of things to put up with, and—who could tell what the future would be?—maybe he would have still more to put up with. Mr. Golyadkin senior protested against this, and began to maintain that one must put one's faith in God. His guest entirely agreed, observing that there was, of course, no one like God. At this point Mr. Golyadkin senior observed that in certain respects the Turks were right in calling upon God even in their sleep. Then, though disagreeing with certain learned professors in the slanders they had promulgated against the Turkish prophet Mahomet and recognizing him as a great politician in his own line, Mr. Golyadkin passed to a very interesting description of an Algerian barber's shop which he had read in a book of miscellanies. The friends laughed heartily at the simplicity of the Turks, but paid due tribute to their fanaticism, which they ascribed to opium. . . . At last the guest began undressing, and thinking in the kindness of his heart that very likely he hadn't even a decent shirt, Mr. Golyadkin went behind the screen to avoid embarrassing a man who had suffered enough, and partly to reassure himself as far as possible about Petrushka, to sound him, to cheer him up if he could, to be kind to the fellow so that every one might be happy and that everything might be pleasant all round. It must be remarked that Petrushka still rather bothered Mr. Golyadkin.

"You go to bed now, Pyotr," Mr. Golyadkin said blandly, going into his servant's domain; "you go to bed now and wake me up at eight o'clock. Do you understand, Petrushka?"

Mr. Golyadkin spoke with exceptional softness and friendliness. But Petrushka remained mute. He was busy making his bed, and did not even turn round to face his master, which he ought to have done out of simple respect.

"Did you hear what I said, Pyotr?" Mr. Golyadkin went on. "You go to bed now and wake me to-morrow at eight o'clock; do you understand?"

"Why, I know that; what's the use of telling me?" Petrushka grumbled to himself.

"Well, that's right, Petrushka; I only mentioned it that you might be happy and at rest. Now we are all happy, so I want you, too, to be happy and satisfied. And now I wish you good-night. Sleep, Petrushka, sleep; we all have to work. . . . Don't think anything amiss, my man . . ." Mr. Golyadkin began, but stopped short. "Isn't this too much?" he thought. "Haven't I gone too far? That's how it always is; I always overdo things."

Our hero felt much dissatisfied with himself as he left Petrushka. He was, besides, rather wounded by Petrushka's grumpiness and rudeness. "One jests with the rascal, his master does him too much honour, and the rascal does not feel it," thought Mr. Golyadkin. "But there, that's the nasty way of all that sort of people!"

Somewhat shaken, he went back to his room, and, seeing that his guest had settled himself for the night, he sat down on the edge of his bed for a minute.

"Come, you must own, Yasha," he began to whisper, wagging his head, "you're a rascal, you know; what a way you've treated me! You see, you've got my name, do you know that?" he went on, jesting in a rather familiar way with his visitor. At last, saying a friendly good-night to him, Mr. Golyadkin began preparing for the night. The visitor meanwhile began snoring. Mr. Golyadkin in his turn got into bed, laughing and whispering to himself: "You are drunk to-day, my dear fellow, Yakov Petrovitch, you rascal, you old Golyadkin—what a surname to have! Why, what are you so pleased about? You'll be crying to-morrow, you know, you sniveller; what am I to do with you?"

At this point a rather strange sensation pervaded Mr. Golyadkin's whole being, something like doubt or remorse.

"I've been over-excited and let myself go," he thought; "now I've a noise in my head and I'm drunk; I couldn't restrain myself, ass that I am! and I've been babbling bushels of nonsense, and, like a rascal, I was planning to be so sly. Of course, to forgive and forget injuries is the height of virtue; but it's a bad thing, nevertheless! Yes, that's so!"

At this point Mr. Golyadkin got up, took a candle and went on tiptoe to look once more at his sleeping guest. He stood over him for a long time, meditating deeply.

"An unpleasant picture! A burlesque, a regular burlesque, and that's the fact of the matter!"

At last Mr. Golyadkin settled down finally. There was a humming, a buzzing, a ringing in his head. He grew more and more drowsy . . . tried to think about something, to remember something very interesting, to decide something very important, some delicate question—but could not. Sleep descended upon his devoted head, and he slept as people generally do sleep who are not used to drinking and have consumed five glasses of punch at some festive gathering.

CHAPTER VIII

MR. GOLYADKIN woke up next morning at eight o'clock as usual; as soon as he was awake he recalled all the adventures of the previous evening—and frowned as he recalled them. "Ugh, I did play the fool last night!" he thought, sitting up and glancing at his visitor's bed. But what was his amazement when he saw in the room no trace, not only of his visitor, but even of the bed on which his visitor had slept!

"What does it mean?" Mr. Golyadkin almost shrieked. "What can it be? What does this new circumstance portend?"

While Mr. Golyadkin was gazing in open-mouthed bewilderment at the empty spot, the door creaked and Petrushka came in with the tea-tray.

"Where, where?" our hero said in a voice hardly audible, pointing to the place which had been occupied by his visitor the night before.

At first Petrushka made no answer and did not look at his master, but fixed his eyes upon the corner to the right till Mr. Golyadkin felt compelled to look into that corner too. After a brief silence, however, Petrushka in a rude and husky voice answered that his master was not at home.

"You idiot; why I'm your master, Petrushka!" said Mr. Golyadkin in a breaking voice, looking open-eyed at his servant.

Petrushka made no reply, but he gave Mr. Golyadkin such a look that the latter crimsoned to his ears—looked at him with an insulting reproachfulness almost equivalent to open abuse. Mr. Golyadkin was utterly flabbergasted, as the saying is. At last Petrushka explained that the *other one* had gone away an hour and a half ago, and would not wait. His answer, of course, sounded truthful and probable; it was evident that Petrushka was not lying; that his insulting look and the phrase the *other one* employed by him were only the result of the disgusting circumstance with which he was already familiar, but still he understood, though dimly, that something was wrong, and that destiny had some other surprise, not altogether a pleasant one, in store for him.

"All right, we shall see," he thought to himself. "We shall see in due time; we'll get to the bottom of all this. . . . Oh, Lord, have mercy upon us!" he moaned in conclusion, in quite a different voice. "And why did I invite him, to what end did I do all that? Why, I am thrusting my head into their thievish noose myself; I am tying the noose with my own hands. Ach, you fool, you fool! You can't resist babbling like some silly boy, some chancery clerk, some wretched creature of no class at all, some rag, some rotten dishclout; you're a gossip, an old woman! . . . Oh, all ye saints! And he wrote verses, the rogue, and expressed his love for me! How could . . . How can I show him the door in a polite way if he turns up again, the rogue? Of course, there are all sorts of ways and means. I can say this is how it is, my salary being so limited. . . . Or scare him off in some way saying that, taking this and that into consideration, I am forced to make clear . . . that he would have to pay an equal share of the cost of board and lodging, and pay the money in advance. H'm! No, damn it all, no! That would be degrading to me. It's not quite delicate! Couldn't I do something like this: suggest to Petrushka that he should annoy him in some way, should be disrespectful, be rude, and get rid of him in that way. Set them at each other in some way. . . . No, damn it all, no! It's dangerous and again, if one looks at it from that point of view—it's not the right thing at all! Not the right thing at all! but there, even if he doesn't come, it will be a bad look-out, too! I babbled to him last night! . . . Ach, it's a bad look-out, a bad look-out! Ach, we're in a bad way! Oh, I'm a cursed fool, a cursed fool! You can't train yourself to behave as you ought, you can't conduct yourself reasonably. Well, what if he comes, and refuses. And God grant he may come! I should be very glad if he did come. . . ."

Such were Mr. Golyadkin's reflections as he swallowed his tea and glanced continually at the clock on the wall.

"It's a quarter to nine; it's time to go. And something will happen! What will there be there? I should like to know what exactly lies hidden in this—that is, the object, the aim, and the various intrigues. It would be a good thing to find out what all these people are plotting, and what will be their first step. . . ."

Mr. Golyadkin could endure it no longer. He threw down his unfinished pipe, dressed and set off for the office, anxious to ward off the danger if possible and to reassure himself about everything by his presence in person. There was danger: he knew himself that there was danger.

"We . . . will get to the bottom of it," said Mr. Golyadkin, taking off his coat and goloshes in the entry. "We'll go into all these matters immediately."

Making up his mind to act in this way, our hero put himself to rights, assumed a correct and official air, and was just about to pass into the adjoining room, when suddenly, in the very doorway, he jostled against his acquaintance of the day before, his friend and companion. Mr. Golyadkin junior seemed not to notice Mr. Golyadkin senior, though they met almost nose to nose. Mr. Golyadkin junior seemed to be busy, to be hastening somewhere, was breathless; he had such an official, such a business-like air that it seemed as though any one could read in his face: 'Entrusted with a special commission.' . . .

"Oh, it's you, Yakov Petrovitch!" said our hero, clutching the hand of his last night's visitor.

"Presently, presently, excuse me, tell me about it afterwards," cried Mr. Golyadkin junior, dashing on.

"But, excuse me; I believe, Yakov Petrovitch, you wanted . . ."

"What is it? Make haste and explain."

At this point his visitor of the previous night halted as though reluctantly and against his will, and put his ear almost to Mr. Golyadkin's nose.

"I must tell you, Yakov Petrovitch, that I am surprised at your behaviour . . . behaviour which seemingly I could not have expected at all."

"There's a proper form for everything. Go to his Excellency's secretary and then appeal in the proper way to the directors of the office. Have you got your petition?"

"You . . . I really don't know, Yakov Petrovitch! You simply amaze me, Yakov Petrovitch! You certainly don't recognize me or, with your characteristic gaiety, you are joking."

"Oh, it's you," said Mr. Golyadkin junior, seeming only now to recognize Mr. Golyadkin senior. "So it's you? Well, have you had a good night?"

Then, smiling a little—a formal and conventional smile, by no means the sort of smile that was befitting (for, after all, he owed a debt of gratitude to Mr. Golyadkin senior)—smiling this formal and conventional smile, Mr. Golyadkin junior added that he was very glad Mr. Golyadkin senior had had a good night; then he made a slight bow and shuffling a little with his feet, looked to the right, and to the left, then dropped his eyes to the floor, made for the side door and muttering in a hurried whisper that he had a special commission, dashed into the next room. He vanished like an apparition.

"Well, this is queer!" muttered our hero, petrified for a moment; "this is queer! This is a strange circumstance."

At this point Mr. Golyadkin felt as though he had pins and needles all over him.

"However," he went on to himself, as he made his way to his department, "however, I spoke long ago of such a circumstance: I had a presentiment long ago that he had a special commission. Why, I said yesterday that the man must certainly be employed on some special commission."

"Have you finished copying out the document you had yesterday, Yakov Petrovitch," Anton Antonovitch Syetotchkin asked Mr. Golyadkin, when the latter was seated beside him. "Have you got it here?"

"Yes," murmured Mr. Golyadkin, looking at the head clerk with a rather helpless glance.

"That's right! I mention it because Andrey Filippovitch has asked for it twice. I'll be bound his Excellency wants it. . . ."

"Yes, it's finished. . . ."

"Well, that's all right then."

"I believe, Anton Antonovitch, I have always performed my duties properly. I'm always scrupulous over the work entrusted to me by my superiors, and I attend to it conscientiously."

"Yes. Why, what do you mean by that?"

"I mean nothing, Anton Antonovitch. I only want to explain, Anton Antonovitch, that I . . . that is, I meant to express that spite and malice sometimes spare no person whatever in their search for their daily and revolting food. . . ."

"Excuse me, I don't quite understand you. What person are you alluding to?"

"I only meant to say, Anton Antonovitch, that I'm seeking the straight path and I scorn going to work in a roundabout way. That I am not one to intrigue, and that, if I may be allowed to say so, I may very justly be proud of it. . . ."

"Yes. That's quite so, and to the best of my comprehension I thoroughly endorse your remarks; but allow me to tell you, Yakov Petrovitch, that personalities are not quite permissible in good society, that I, for instance, am ready to put up with anything behind my back—for every one's abused behind his back—but to my face, if you please, my good sir, I don't allow any one to be impudent. I've grown grey in the government service, sir, and I don't allow any one to be impudent to me in my old age. . . ."

"No, Anton Antonovitch . . . you see, Anton Antonovitch . . . you haven't quite caught my meaning. To be sure, Anton Antonovitch, I for my part could only think it an honour. . . ."

"Well, then, I ask your pardon too. We've been brought up in the old school. And it's too late for us to learn your newfangled ways. I believe we've had understanding enough for the service of our country up to now. As you are aware, sir, I have an order of merit for twenty-five years' irreproachable service. . . ."

"I feel it, Anton Antonovitch, on my side, too, I quite feel all that. But I didn't mean that, I am speaking of a mask, Anton Antonovitch. . . ."

"A mask?"

"Again you . . . I am apprehensive that you are taking this, too, in a wrong sense, that is the sense of my remarks, as you say yourself, Anton Antonovitch. I am simply enunciating a theory, that is, I am advancing the idea, Anton Antonovitch, that persons who wear a mask have become far from uncommon, and that nowadays it is hard to recognize the man beneath the mask. . . ."

"Well, do you know, it's not altogether so hard. Sometimes it's fairly easy. Sometimes one need not go far to look for it."

"No, you know, Anton Antonovitch, I say, I say of myself, that I, for instance, do not put on a mask except when there is need of it; that is simply at carnival time or at some festive gathering, speaking in the literal sense; but that I do not wear a mask before people in daily life, speaking in another less obvious sense. That's what I meant to say, Anton Antonovitch."

"Oh, well, but we must drop all this, for now I've no time to spare," said Anton Antonovitch, getting up from his seat and collecting some papers in order to report upon them to his Excellency. "Your business, as I imagine, will be explained in due course without delay. You will see for yourself whom you should censure and whom you should blame, and thereupon I humbly beg you to spare me from further private explanations and arguments which interfere with my work. . . ."

"No, Anton Antonovitch," Mr. Golyadkin, turning a little pale, began to the retreating figure of Anton Antonovitch; "I had no thought of the kind."

"What does it mean?" our hero went on to himself, when he was left alone; "what quarter is the wind in now, and what is one to make of this new turn?"

At the very time when our bewildered and half-crushed hero was setting himself to solve this new question, there was a sound of movement and bustle in the next room, the door opened and Andrey Filippovitch, who had been on some business in his Excellency's study, appeared breathless in the doorway, and called to Mr. Golyadkin. Knowing what was wanted and anxious not to keep Andrey Filippovitch waiting, Mr. Golyadkin leapt up from his seat, and as was fitting immediately bustled for all he was worth getting the manuscript that was required finally neat and ready and preparing to follow the manuscript and Andrey Filippovitch into his Excellency's study. Suddenly, almost slipping under the arm of Andrey Filippovitch, who was standing right in the doorway, Mr. Golyadkin junior darted into the room in breathless haste and bustle, with a solemn and resolutely official air; he bounded straight up to Mr. Golyadkin senior, who was expecting nothing less than such a visitation.

"The papers, Yakov Petrovitch, the papers . . . his Excellency has been pleased to ask for them; have you got them ready?" Mr. Golyadkin senior's friend whispered in a hurried undertone. "Andrey Filippovitch is waiting for you. . . ."

"I know he is waiting without your telling me," said Mr. Golyadkin senior, also in a hurried whisper.

"No, Yakov Petrovitch, I did not mean that; I did not mean that at all, Yakov Petrovitch, not that at all; I sympathize with you, Yakov Petrovitch, and am moved by genuine interest."

"Which I most humbly beg you to spare me. Allow me, allow me . . ."

"You'll put it in an envelope, of course, Yakov Petrovitch, and you'll put a mark in the third page; allow me, Yakov Petrovitch. . . ."

"You allow me, if you please. . . ."

"But, I say, there's a blot here, Yakov Petrovitch; did you know there was a blot here? . . ."

At this point Andrey Filippovitch called Yakov Petrovitch a second time.

"One moment, Andrey Filippovitch, I'm only just . . . Do you understand Russian, sir?"

"It would be best to take it out with a penknife, Yakov Petrovitch. You had better rely upon me; you had better not touch it yourself, Yakov Petrovitch, rely upon me—I'll do it with a penknife. . . ."

Andrey Filippovitch called Mr. Golyadkin a third time.

"But, allow me, where's the blot? I don't think there's a blot at all."

"It's a huge blot. Here it is! Here, allow me, I saw it here . . . you just let me, Yakov Petrovitch, I'll just touch it with the penknife, I'll scratch it out with the penknife from true-hearted sympathy. There, like this; see, it's done."

At this point, and quite unexpectedly, Mr. Golyadkin junior overpowered Mr. Golyadkin senior in the momentary struggle that had arisen between them, and so, entirely against the latter's will, suddenly, without rhyme or reason, took possession of the document required by the authorities, and instead of scratching it out with the penknife in true-hearted sympathy as he had perfidiously promised Mr. Golyadkin senior, hurriedly rolled it up, put it under his arm, in two bounds was beside Andrey Filippovitch, who noticed none of his manœuvres, and flew with the latter into the Director's room. Mr. Golyadkin remained as though riveted to the spot, holding the penknife in his hand and apparently on the point of scratching something out with it. . . .

Our hero could not yet grasp his new position. He could not at once recover himself. He felt the blow, but thought that it was somehow all right. In terrible, indescribable misery he tore himself at last from his seat, rushed straight to the Director's room, imploring heaven on the way that it might somehow all be arranged satisfactorily and so would be all right. . . . In the furthermost room, which adjoined the Director's private room, he ran straight upon Andrey Filippovitch in company with his namesake. Both of them were coming back; Mr. Golyadkin moved aside. Andrey Filippovitch was talking with a good-humoured smile, Mr. Golyadkin senior's namesake was smiling, too, fawning upon Andrey Filippovitch and tripping about at a respectful distance from him, and was whispering something in his ear with a delighted air, to which Andrey Filippovitch assented with a gracious nod. In a flash our hero grasped the whole position. The fact was that the work had surpassed his Excellency's expectations (as he learnt afterwards) and was finished punctually by the time it was needed. His Excellency was extremely pleased with it. It was even said that his Excellency had said "Thank you" to Mr. Golyadkin junior, had thanked him warmly, had said that he would remember it on occasion and would never forget it. . . . Of course, the first thing Mr. Golyadkin did was to protest, to protest with the utmost vigour of which he was capable. Pale as death, and hardly knowing what he was doing, he rushed up to Andrey Filippovitch. But the latter, hearing that Mr. Golyadkin's business was a private matter, refused to listen, observing firmly that he had not a minute to spare even for his own affairs.

The curtness of his tone and his refusal struck Mr. Golyadkin.

"I had better, perhaps, try in another quarter. . . . I had better appeal to Anton Antonovitch."

But to his disappointment Anton Antonovitch was not available either: he, too, was busy over something somewhere!

"Ah, it was not without design that he asked me to spare him explanation and discussion!" thought our hero. "This was what the old rogue had in his mind! In that case I shall simply make bold to approach his Excellency."

Still pale and feeling that his brain was in a complete ferment, greatly perplexed as to what he ought to decide to do, Mr. Golyadkin sat down on the edge of the chair. "It would have been a great deal better if it had all been just nothing," he kept incessantly thinking to himself. "Indeed, such a mysterious business was utterly improbable. In the first place, it was nonsense, and secondly it could not happen. Most likely it was imagination, or something else happened, and not what really did happen; or perhaps I went myself . . . and somehow mistook myself for some one else . . . in short, it's an utterly impossible thing."

Mr. Golyadkin had no sooner made up his mind that it was an utterly impossible thing than Mr. Golyadkin junior flew into the room with papers in both hands as well as under his arm. Saying two or three words about business to Andrey Filippovitch as he passed, exchanging remarks with one, polite greetings with another, and familiarities with a third, Mr. Golyadkin junior, having apparently no time to waste, seemed on the point of leaving the room, but luckily for Mr. Golyadkin senior he stopped near the door to say a few words as he passed two or three clerks who were at work there. Mr. Golyadkin senior rushed straight at him. As soon as Mr. Golyadkin junior saw Mr. Golyadkin senior's movement he began immediately, with great uneasiness, looking about him to make his escape. But our hero already held his last night's guest by the sleeve. The clerks surrounding the two titular councillors stepped back and waited with curiosity to see what would happen. The senior titular councillor realized that public opinion was not on his side, he realized that they were intriguing against him: which made it all the more necessary to hold his own now. The moment was a decisive one.

"Well!" said Mr. Golyadkin junior, looking rather impatiently at Mr. Golyadkin senior.

The latter could hardly breathe.

"I don't know," he began, "in what way to make plain to you the strangeness of your behaviour, sir."

"Well. Go on." At this point Mr. Golyadkin junior turned round and winked to the clerks standing round, as though to give them to understand that a comedy was beginning.

"The impudence and shamelessness of your manners with me, sir, in the present case, unmasks your true character . . . better than any words of mine could do. Don't rely on your trickery: it is worthless. . . ."

"Come, Yakov Petrovitch, tell me now, how did you spend the night?" answered Mr. Golyadkin junior, looking Mr. Golyadkin senior straight in the eye.

"You forget yourself, sir," said the titular councillor, completely flabbergasted, hardly able to feel the floor under his feet. "I trust that you will take a different tone. . . ."

"My darling!" exclaimed Mr. Golyadkin junior, making a rather unseemly grimace at Mr. Golyadkin senior, and suddenly, quite unexpectedly, under the pretence of caressing him, he pinched his chubby cheek with two fingers.

Our hero grew as hot as fire. . . . As soon as Mr. Golyadkin junior noticed that his opponent, quivering in every limb, speechless with rage, as red as a lobster, and exasperated beyond all endurance, might actually be driven to attack him, he promptly and in the most shameless way hastened to be beforehand with his victim. Patting him two or three times on the cheek, tickling him two or three times, playing with him for a few seconds in this way while his victim stood rigid and beside himself with fury to the no little diversion of the young men standing round, Mr. Golyadkin junior ended with a most revolting shamelessness by giving Mr. Golyadkin senior a poke in his rather prominent stomach, and with a most venomous and suggestive smile said to him: "You're mischievous, brother Yakov, you are mischievous! We'll be sly, you and I, Yakov Petrovitch, we'll be sly."

Then, and before our hero could gradually come to himself after the last attack, Mr. Golyadkin junior (with a little smile beforehand to the spectators standing round) suddenly assumed a most businesslike, busy and official air, dropped his eyes to the floor and, drawing himself in, shrinking together, and pronouncing rapidly "on a special commission" he cut a caper with his short leg, and darted away into the next room. Our hero could not believe his eyes and was still unable to pull himself together. . . .

At last he roused himself. Recognizing in a flash that he was ruined, in a sense annihilated, that he had disgraced himself and sullied his reputation, that he had been turned into ridicule and treated with contempt in the presence of spectators, that he had been treacherously insulted, by one whom he had looked on only the day before as his greatest and most trustworthy friend, that he had been put to utter confusion, Mr. Golyadkin senior rushed in pursuit of his enemy. At the moment he would not even think of the witnesses of his ignominy.

"They're all in a conspiracy together," he said to himself; "they stand by each other and set each other on to attack me." After taking a dozen steps, however, our hero perceived clearly that all pursuit would be vain and useless, and so he turned back. "You won't get away," he thought, "you will get caught one day; the wolf will have to pay for the sheep's tears."

With ferocious composure and the most resolute determination Mr. Golyadkin went up to his chair and sat down upon it. "You won't escape," he said again.

Now it was not a question of passive resistance: there was determination and pugnacity in the air, and any one who had seen how Mr. Golyadkin at that moment, flushed and scarcely able to restrain his excitement, stabbed his pen into the inkstand and with what fury he began scribbling on the paper, could be certain beforehand that the matter would not pass off like this, and could not end in a simple, womanish way. In the depth of his soul he formed a resolution, and in the depth of his heart swore to carry it out. To tell the truth he still did not quite know how to act, or rather did not know at all, but never mind, that did not matter!

"Imposture and shamelessness do not pay nowadays, sir. Imposture and shamelessness, sir, lead to no good, but lead to the halter. Grishka Otrepyov was the only one, sir, who gained by imposture, deceiving the blind people and even that not for long."

In spite of this last circumstance Mr. Golyadkin proposed to wait till such time as the mask should fall from certain persons and something should be made manifest. For this it was necessary, in the first place, that office hours should be over as soon as possible, and till then our hero proposed to take no step. Then, when office hours were over, he would take one step. He knew then how he must act after taking that step, how to arrange his whole plan of action, to abase the horn of arrogance and crush the snake gnawing the dust in contemptible impotence. To allow himself to be treated like a rag used for wiping dirty boots, Mr. Golyadkin could not. He could not consent to that, especially in the present case. Had it not been for that last insult, our hero might have, perhaps, brought himself to control his anger; he might, perhaps, have been silent, have submitted and not have protested too obstinately; he would just have disputed a little, have made a slight complaint, have proved that he was in the right, then he would have given way a little, then, perhaps, he would have given way a little more, then he would have come round altogether, then, especially when the opposing party solemnly admitted that he was right, perhaps, he would have overlooked it completely, would even have been a little touched, there might even, perhaps—who could tell—spring up a new, close, warm friendship, on an even broader basis than the friendship of last night, so that this friendship might, in the end, completely eclipse the unpleasantness of the rather unseemly resemblance of the two individuals, so that both the titular councillors might be highly delighted, and might go on living till they were a hundred, and so on. To tell the whole truth, Mr. Golyadkin began to regret a little that he had stood up for himself and his rights, and had at once come in for unpleasantness in consequence.

"Should he give in," thought Mr. Golyadkin, "say he was joking, I would forgive him. I would forgive him even more if he would acknowledge it aloud. But I won't let myself be treated like a rag. And I have not allowed even persons very different from him to treat me so, still less will I permit a depraved person to attempt it. I am not a rag. I am not a rag, sir!"

In short, our hero made up his mind; "You're in fault yourself, sir!" he thought. He made up his mind to protest, and to protest with all his might to the very last. That was the sort of man he was! He could not consent to allow himself to be insulted, still less to allow himself to be treated as a rag, and, above all, to allow a thoroughly vicious man to treat him so. No quarrelling, however, no quarrelling! Possibly if some one wanted, if some one, for instance, actually insisted on turning Mr. Golyadkin into a rag, he might have done so, might have done so without opposition or punishment (Mr. Golyadkin was himself conscious of this at times), and he would have been a rag and not Golyadkin—yes, a nasty, filthy rag; but that rag would not have been a simple rag, it would have been a rag possessed of dignity, it would have been a rag possessed of feelings and sentiments, even though dignity was defence-less and feelings could not assert themselves, and lay hidden deep down in the filthy folds of the rag, still the feelings were there. . .

The hours dragged on incredibly slowly; at last it struck four. Soon after, all got up and, following the head of the department, moved each on his homeward way. Mr. Golyadkin mingled with the crowd; he kept a vigilant look out, and did not lose sight of the man he wanted. At last our hero saw that his friend ran up to the office attendants who handed the clerks their overcoats, and hung about near them waiting for his in his usual nasty way. The minute was a decisive one. Mr. Golyadkin forced his way somehow through the crowd and, anxious not to be left behind, he, too, began fussing about his overcoat. But Mr. Golyadkin's friend and companion was given his overcoat first because on this occa-sion, too, he had succeeded, as he always did, in making up to them, whispering something to them, cringing upon them and getting round them.

After putting on his overcoat, Mr. Golyadkin junior glanced ironi-cally at Mr. Golyadkin senior, acting in this way openly and defiantly, looked about him with his characteristic insolence, finally he tripped to and fro among the other clerks—no doubt in order to leave a good impression on them—said a word to one, whispered something to another, respectfully accosted a third, directed a smile at a fourth, gave his hand to a fifth, and gaily darted downstairs. Mr. Golyadkin senior flew after him, and to his inexpressible delight overtook him on the last step, and seized him by the collar of his overcoat. It seemed as though Mr. Golyadkin junior was a little disconcerted, and he looked about him with a helpless air.

"What do you mean by this?" he whispered to Mr. Golyadkin at last, in a weak voice.

"Sir, if you are a gentleman, I trust that you remember our friendly relations yesterday," said our hero.

"Ah, yes! Well? Did you sleep well?"

Fury rendered Mr. Golyadkin senior speechless for a moment.

"I slept well, sir . . . but allow me to tell you, sir, that you are playing a very complicated game. . . ."

"Who says so? My enemies say that," answered abruptly the man who called himself Mr. Golyadkin, and saying this, he unexpectedly freed himself from the feeble hand of the real Mr. Golyadkin. As soon as he was free he rushed away from the stairs, looked around him, saw a cab, ran up to it, got in, and in one moment vanished from Mr. Golyadkin senior's sight. The despairing titular councillor, abandoned by all, gazed about him, but there was no other cab. He tried to run, but his legs gave way under him. With a look of open-mouthed astonishment on his countenance, feeling crushed and shrivelled up, he leaned helplessly against a lamp post, and remained so for some minutes in the middle of the pavement. It seemed as though all were over for Mr. Golyadkin.

CHAPTER IX

EVERYTHING, apparently, and even nature itself, seemed up in arms against Mr. Golyadkin; but he was still on his legs and unconquered; he felt that he was unconquered. He was ready to struggle. He rubbed his hands with such feeling and such energy when he recovered from his first amazement that it could be deduced from his very air that he would not give in. Yet the danger was imminent; it was evident; Mr. Golyadkin felt it; but how to grapple with it, with this danger?—that was the question. The thought even flashed through Mr. Golyadkin's mind for a moment, "After all, why not leave it so, simply give it up? Why, what is it? Why, it's nothing. I'll keep apart as though it were not I," thought Mr. Golyadkin. "I'll let it all pass; it's not I, and that's all about it; he's separate too, maybe he'll give it up too; he'll hang about, the rascal, he'll hang about. He'll come back and give it up again. That's how it will be! I'll take it meekly. And, indeed, where is the danger? Come, what danger is there? I should like any one to tell me where the danger lies in this business. It is a trivial affair. An everyday affair. . . ."

At this point Mr. Golyadkin's tongue failed; the words died away on his lips; he even swore at himself for this thought; he convicted himself on the spot of abjectness, of cowardice for having this thought; things were no forwarder, however. He felt that to make up his mind to some course of action was absolutely necessary for him at the moment; he even felt that he would have given a great deal to any one who could have told him what he must decide to do. Yes, but how could he guess what? Though, indeed, he had no time to guess. In any case, that he might lose no time he took a cab and dashed home.

"Well? What are you feeling now?" he wondered; "what are you graciously pleased to be thinking of, Yakov Petrovitch? What are you doing? What are you doing now, you rogue, you rascal? You've brought yourself to this plight, and now you are weeping and whimpering!"

So Mr. Golyadkin taunted himself as he jolted along in the vehicle. To taunt himself and so to irritate his wounds was, at this time, a great satisfaction to Mr. Golyadkin, almost a voluptuous enjoyment.

"Well," he thought, "if some magician were to turn up now, or if it could come to pass in some official way and I were told: 'Give a finger of your right hand, Golyadkin—and it's a bargain with you; there shall not be the other Golyadkin, and you will be happy, only you won't have your finger'—yes, I would sacrifice my finger, I would certainly sacrifice it, I would sacrifice it without winking. . . . The devil take it all!" the despairing titular councillor cried at last. "Why, what is it all for? Well, it all had to be; yes, it absolutely had to; yes, just this had to be, as though nothing else were possible! And it was all right at first. Every one was pleased and happy. But there, it had to be! There's nothing to be gained by talking, though; you must act."

And so, almost resolved upon some action, Mr. Golyadkin reached home, and without a moment's delay snatched up his pipe and, sucking at it with all his might and puffing out clouds of smoke to right and to left, he began pacing up and down the room in a state of violent excitement. Meanwhile, Petrushka began laying the table. At last Mr.

Golyadkin made up his mind completely, flung aside his pipe, put on his overcoat, said he would not dine at home and ran out of the flat. Petrushka, panting, overtook him on the stairs, bringing the hat he had forgotten. Mr. Golyadkin took his hat, wanted to say something incidentally to justify himself in Petrushka's eyes that the latter might not think anything particular, such as, "What a queer circumstance! here he forgot his hat—and so on," but as Petrushka walked away at once and would not even look at him, Mr. Golyadkin put on his hat without further explanation, ran downstairs, and repeating to himself that perhaps everything might be for the best, and that affairs would somehow be arranged, though he was conscious among other things of a cold chill right down to his heels, he went out into the street, took a cab and hastened to Andrey Filippovitch's.

"Would it not be better to-morrow, though?" thought Mr. Golyadkin, as he took hold of the bell-rope of Andrey Filippovitch's flat. "And, besides, what can I say in particular? There is nothing particular in it. It's such a wretched affair, yes, it really is wretched, paltry, yes, that is, almost a paltry affair . . . yes, that's what it all is, the incident. . . ." Suddenly Mr. Golyadkin pulled at the bell; the bell rang; footsteps were heard within. . . . Mr. Golyadkin cursed himself on the spot for his hastiness and audacity. His recent unpleasant experiences, which he had almost forgotten over his work, and his encounter with Andrey Filippovitch immediately came back into his mind. But by now it was too late to run away: the door opened. Luckily for Mr. Golyadkin he was informed that Andrey Filippovitch had not returned from the office and had not dined at home.

"I know where he dines: he dines near the Ismailovsky Bridge," thought our hero; and he was immensely relieved. To the footman's inquiry what message he would leave, he said: "It's all right, my good man, I'll look in later," and he even ran downstairs with a certain cheerful briskness. Going out into the street, he decided to dismiss the cab and paid the driver. When the man asked for something extra, saying he had been waiting in the street and had not spared his horse for his honour, he gave him five kopecks extra, and even willingly; and then walked on.

"It really is such a thing," thought Mr. Golyadkin, "that it cannot be left like that; though, if one looks at it that way, looks at it sensibly, why am I hurrying about here, in reality? Well, yes, though, I will go on discussing why I should take a lot of trouble; why I should rush about, exert myself, worry myself and wear myself out. To begin with, the thing's done and there's no recalling it . . . of course, there's no recalling it! Let us put it like this: a man turns up with a satisfactory reference, said to be a capable clerk, of good conduct, only he is a poor man and has suffered many reverses—all sorts of ups and downs—well, poverty is not a crime: so I must stand aside. Why, what nonsense it is! Well, he came; he is so made, the man is so made by nature itself that he is as like another man as though they were two drops of water, as though he were a perfect copy of another man; how could they refuse to take him into the department on that account? If it is fate, if it is only fate, if it is only blind chance that is to blame—is he to be treated like a rag, is he to be refused a job in the office? . . . Why, what would become of justice after that? He is a poor man, hopeless, downcast; it makes one's heart ache: compassion bids one care for him! Yes! There's no denying, there would be a fine set of head officials, if they took the same view as a reprobate like me! What an addlepate I am! I have foolishness enough for a dozen! Yes, yes! They did right, and many thanks to them for being good to a poor, luckless fellow. . . . Why, let us imagine for a moment that we are twins, that we had been born twin brothers, and nothing else—there it is! Well, what of it? Why, nothing! All the clerks can get used to it. . . . And an outsider, coming into our office, would certainly find nothing unseemly or offensive in the circumstance. In fact, there is really something touching in it; to think that the divine Providence created two men exactly alike, and the heads of the department, seeing the divine handiwork, provided for two twins. It would, of course," Mr. Golyadkin went on, drawing a breath and dropping his voice, "it would, of course . . . it would, of course, have been better if there had been . . . if there had been nothing of this touching kindness, and if there had been no twins either. . . . The devil take it all! And what need was there for it? And what was the particular necessity that admitted of no delay! My goodness! The devil has made a mess of it! Besides, he has such a character, too, he's of such a playful, horrid disposition—he's such a scoundrel, he's such a nimble fellow! He's such a toady! Such a lickspittle! He's such a Golyadkin! I daresay he will misconduct himself; yes, he'll disgrace my name, the blackguard! And now I have to look after him and wait upon him! What an infliction! But, after all, what of it? It doesn't matter. Granted, he's a scoundrel, well, let him be a scoundrel, but to make up for it, the other one's honest; so he will be a scoundrel and I'll be honest, and they'll say that this Golyadkin's a rascal, don't take any notice of him, and don't mix him up with the other; but the other one's honest, virtuous, mild, free from malice, always to be relied upon in the service, and worthy of promotion; that's how it is, very good . . . but what if . . . what if they get us mixed up! . . . He is equal to anything! Ah, Lord, have mercy upon us! . . . He will counterfeit a man, he will counterfeit him, the rascal—he will change one man for another as though he were a rag, and not reflect that a man is not a rag. Ach, mercy on us! Ough, what a calamity! . . ."

Reflecting and lamenting in this way, Mr. Golyadkin ran on, regardless of where he was going. He came to his senses in Nevsky Prospect, only owing to the chance that he ran so neatly full-tilt into a passer-by that he saw stars in his eyes. Mr. Golyadkin muttered his excuses without raising his head, and it was only after the passer-by, muttering something far from flattering, had walked a considerable distance away, that he raised his nose and looked about to see where he was and how he had got there. Noticing when he did so that he was close to the restaurant in which he had sat for a while before the dinner-party at Olsufy Ivanovitch's, our hero was suddenly conscious of a pinching and nipping sensation in his stomach; he remembered that he had not dined; he had no prospect of a dinner-party anywhere. And so, without losing precious time, he ran upstairs into the restaurant to have a snack of something as quickly as possible, and to avoid delay by making all the haste he could. And though everything in the restaurant was rather dear, that little circumstance did not on this occasion make Mr. Golyadkin pause, and, indeed, he had no time to pause over such a trifle. In the brightly lighted room the customers were standing in rather a crowd round the counter, upon which lay heaps of all sorts of such edibles as are eaten by well-bred persons at lunch. The waiter scarcely had time to fill glasses, to serve, to take money and give change. Mr. Golyadkin waited for his turn and modestly stretched out his hand for a savoury patty. Retreating into a corner, turning his back on the company and eating with appetite, he went back to the attendant, put down his plate and, knowing the price, took out a ten-kopeck piece and laid the coin on the counter, catching the waiter's eye as though to say, "Look, here's the money, one pie," and so on.

"One rouble ten kopecks is your bill," the waiter filtered through his teeth.

Mr. Golyadkin was a good deal surprised.

"You are speaking to me? . . . I . . . I took one pie, I believe."

"You've had eleven," the man retorted confidently.

"You . . . so it seems to me . . . I believe, you're mistaken. . . . I really took only one pie, I think."

"I counted them; you took eleven. Since you've had them you must pay for them; we don't give anything away for nothing."

Mr. Golyadkin was petrified. "What sorcery is this, what is happening to me?" he wondered. Meanwhile, the man waited for Mr. Golyadkin to make up his mind; people crowded round Mr. Golyadkin; he was already feeling in his pocket for a silver rouble, to pay the full amount at once, to avoid further trouble. "Well, if it was eleven, it was eleven," he thought, turning as red as a lobster. "Why, what does it matter if eleven pies have been eaten? Why, a man's hungry, so he eats eleven pies; well, let him eat, and may it do him good; and there's nothing to wonder at in that, and there's nothing to laugh at. . . ."

At that moment something seemed to stab Mr. Golyadkin. He raised his eyes and—at once he guessed the riddle. He knew what the sorcery was. All his difficulties were solved. . . .

In the doorway of the next room, almost directly behind the waiter and facing Mr. Golyadkin, in the doorway which, till that moment, our hero had taken for a looking-glass, a man was standing—he was standing, Mr. Golyadkin was standing—not the original Mr. Golyadkin, the hero of our story, but the other Mr. Golyadkin, the new Mr. Golyadkin. The second Mr. Golyadkin was apparently in excellent spirits. He smiled to Mr. Golyadkin the first, nodded to him, winked, shuffled his feet a little, and looked as though in another minute he would vanish, would disappear into the next room, and then go out, maybe, by a back way out; and there it would be, and all pursuit would be in vain. In his hand he had the last morsel of the tenth pie, and before Mr. Golyadkin's very eyes he popped it into his mouth and smacked his lips.

"He has impersonated me, the scoundrel!" thought Mr. Golyadkin, flushing hot with shame. "He is not ashamed of the publicity of it! Do they see him? I fancy no one notices him. . . ."

Mr. Golyadkin threw down his rouble as though it burnt his fingers, and without noticing the waiter's insolently significant grin, a smile of triumph and serene power, he extricated himself from the crowd, and rushed away without looking round. "We must be thankful that at least he has not completely compromised any one!" thought Mr. Golyadkin senior. "We must be thankful to him, the brigand, and to fate, that everything was satisfactorily settled. The waiter was rude, that was all. But, after all, he was in the right. One rouble and ten kopecks were owing: so he was in the right. 'We don't give things away for nothing,' he said! Though he might have been more polite, the rascal . . ."

All this Mr. Golyadkin said to himself as he went downstairs to the entrance, but on the last step he stopped suddenly, as though he had been shot, and suddenly flushed till the tears came into his eyes at the insult to his dignity. After standing stockstill for half a minute, he stamped his foot resolutely, at one bound leapt from the step into the street and, without looking round, rushed breathless and unconscious of fatigue back home to his flat in Shestilavotchny Street. When he got home, without changing his coat, though it was his habit to change into an old coat at home, without even stopping to take his pipe, he sat down on the sofa, drew the inkstand towards him, took up a pen, got a sheet of notepaper, and with a hand that trembled from inward excitement, began scribbling the following epistle—

"Dear Sir Yakov Petrovitch!

"I should not take up my pen if my circumstances, and your own action, sir, had not compelled me to that step. Believe me that nothing but necessity would have induced me to enter upon such a discussion with you; and therefore, first of all, I beg you, sir, to look upon this step of mine not as a premeditated design to insult you, but as the inevitable consequence of the circumstance that is a bond between us now."

("I think that's all right, proper, courteous, though not lacking in force and firmness. . . . I don't think there is anything for him to take offence at. Besides, I'm fully within my rights," thought Mr. Golyadkin, reading over what he had written.)

"Your strange and sudden appearance, sir, on a stormy night, after the coarse and unseemly behaviour of my enemies to me, for whom I feel too much contempt even to mention their names, was the starting-point of all the misunderstanding existing between us at the present time. Your obstinate desire to persist in your course of action, sir, and forcibly to enter the circle of my existence and all my relations in practical life, transgresses every limit imposed by the merest politeness and every rule of civilized society. I imagine there is no need, sir, for me to refer to the seizure by you of my papers, and particularly to your taking away my good name, in order to gain the favour of my superiors—favour you have not deserved. There is no need to refer here either to your intentional and insulting refusal of the necessary explanation in regard to us. Finally, to omit nothing, I will not allude here to your last strange, one may even say, your incomprehensible behaviour to me in the coffeehouse. I am far from lamenting over the needless—for me—loss of a rouble; but I cannot help expressing my indignation at the recollection of your public outrage upon me, to the detriment of my honour, and what is more, in the presence of several persons of good breeding, though not belonging to my circle of acquaintance."

("Am I not going too far?" thought Mr. Golyadkin. "Isn't it too much; won't it be too insulting—that taunt about good breeding, for instance? . . . But there, it doesn't matter! I must show him the resoluteness of my character. I might, however, to soften him, flatter him, and butter him up at the end. But there, we shall see.")

"But I should not weary you with my letter, sir, if I were not firmly convinced that the nobility of your sentiments and your open, candid character would suggest to you yourself a means for retrieving all lapses and returning everything to its original position.

"With full confidence I venture to rest assured that you will not take my letter in a sense derogatory to yourself, and at the same time that you will not refuse to explain yourself expressly on this occasion by letter, sending the same by my man.

"In expectation of your reply, I have the honour, dear sir, to remain,
                              "Your humble servant,
                                             "Y. GOLYADKIN."

"Well, that is quite all right. The thing's done, it has come to letter-writing. But who is to blame for that? He is to blame himself: by his own action he reduces a man to the necessity of resorting to epistolary composition. And I am within my rights. . . ."

Reading over his letter for the last time, Mr. Golyadkin folded it up, sealed it and called Petrushka. Petrushka came in looking, as usual, sleepy and cross about something.

"You will take this letter, my boy . . . do you understand?"

Petrushka did not speak.

"You will take it to the department; there you must find the secretary on duty, Vahramyev. He is the one on duty to-day. Do you understand that?"

"I understand."

"'I understand'! He can't even say, 'I understand, sir!' You must ask for the secretary, Vahramyev, and tell him that your master desired you to send his regards, and humbly requests him to refer to the address book of our office and find out where the titular councilor, Golyadkin, is living?"

Petrushka remained mute, and, as Mr. Golyadkin fancied, smiled.

"Well, so you see, Pyotr, you have to ask him for the address, and find out where the new clerk, Golyadkin, lives."

"Yes,"

"You must ask for the address and then take this letter there. Do you understand?"

"I understand."

"If there . . . where you have to take the letter, that gentleman to whom you have to give the letter, that Golyadkin . . . What are you laughing at, you blockhead?"

"What is there to laugh at? What is it to me! I wasn't doing anything, sir. It's not for the likes of us to laugh. . . ."

"Oh, well . . . if that gentleman should ask, 'How is your master, how is he'; if he . . . well, if he should ask you anything—you hold your tongue, and answer, 'My master is all right, and begs you for an answer to his letter.' Do you understand?"

"Yes, sir."

"Well, then, say, 'My master is all right and quite well,' say, 'and is just getting ready to pay a call: and he asks you,' say, 'for an answer in writing.' Do you understand?"

"Yes."

"Well, go along, then.

"Why, what a bother I have with this blockhead too! He's laughing, and there's nothing to be done. What's he laughing at? I've lived to see trouble. Here I've lived like this to see trouble. Though perhaps it may all turn out for the best. . . . That rascal will be loitering about for the next two hours now, I expect; he'll go off somewhere else. . . . There's no sending him anywhere. What a misery it is! . . . What misery has come upon me!"

Feeling his troubles to the full, our hero made up his mind to remain passive for two hours till Petrushka returned. For an hour of the time he walked about the room, smoked, then put aside his pipe and sat down to a book, then he lay down on the sofa, then took up his pipe again, then again began running about the room. He tried to think things over but was absolutely unable to think about anything. At last the agony of remaining passive reached the climax and Mr. Golyadkin made up his mind to take a step. "Petrushka will come in another hour," he thought. "I can give the key to the porter, and I myself can, so to speak . . . I can investigate the matter: I shall investigate the matter in my own way."

Without loss of time, in haste to investigate the matter, Mr. Golyadkin took his hat, went out of the room, locked up his flat, went in to the porter, gave him the key, together with ten kopecks—Mr. Golyadkin had become extraordinarily freehanded of late—and rushed off. Mr. Golyadkin went first on foot to the Ismailovsky Bridge. It took him half an hour to get there. When he reached the goal of his journey he went straight into the yard of the house so familiar to him, and glanced up at the windows of the civil councillor Berendyev's flat. Except for three windows hung with red curtains all the rest was dark.

"Olsufy Ivanovitch has no visitors to-day," thought Mr. Golyadkin; "they must all be staying at home to-day."

After standing for some time in the yard, our hero tried to decide on some course of action. But he was apparently not destined to reach a decision. Mr. Golyadkin changed his mind, and with a wave of his hand went back into the street.

"No, there's no need for me to go to-day. What could I do here? . . .
No, I'd better, so to speak . . . I'll investigate the matter personally."

Coming to this conclusion, Mr. Golyadkin rushed off to his office.
He had a long way to go. It was horribly muddy, besides, and the wet
snow lay about in thick drifts. But it seemed as though difficulty did not
exist for our hero at the moment. He was drenched through, it is true,
and he was a good deal spattered with mud.

"But that's no matter, so long as the object is obtained."

And Mr. Golyadkin certainly was nearing his goal. The dark mass of
the huge government building stood up black before his eyes.

"Stay," he thought; "where am I going, and what am I going to do
here? Suppose I do find out where he lives? Meanwhile, Petrushka will
certainly have come back and brought me the answer. I am only wasting my precious time, I am simply wasting my time. Though shouldn't
I, perhaps, go in and see Vahramyev? But, no, I'll go later. . . . Ech!
There was no need to have gone out at all. But, there, it's my temperament! I've a knack of always seizing a chance of rushing ahead of things,
whether there is a need to or not. . . . H'm! . . . what time is it? It must
be nine by now. Petrushka might come and not find me at home. It was
pure folly on my part to go out . . . Ech, it is really a nuisance!"

Sincerely acknowledging that he had been guilty of an act of folly,
our hero ran back to Shestilavotchny Street. He arrived there, weary
and exhausted. From the porter he learned that Petrushka had not
dreamed of turning up yet.

"To be sure! I foresaw it would be so," thought our hero; "and meanwhile it's nine o'clock. Ech, he's such a good-for-nothing chap! He's
always drinking somewhere! Mercy on us! What a day has fallen to my
miserable lot!"

Reflecting in this way, Mr. Golyadkin unlocked his flat, got a light,
took off his outdoor things, lighted his pipe and, tired, worn-out,
exhausted and hungry, lay down on the sofa and waited for Petrushka.
The candle burnt dimly; the light flickered on the wall. . . . Mr. Golyadkin gazed and gazed, and thought and thought, and fell asleep at last,
worn out.

It was late when he woke up. The candle had almost burnt down, was
smoking and on the point of going out. Mr. Golyadkin jumped up,
shook himself, and remembered it all, absolutely all. Behind the screen
he heard Petrushka snoring lustily. Mr. Golyadkin rushed to the window—not a light anywhere. He opened the movable pane—all was
still; the city was asleep as though it were dead: so it must have been two

or three o'clock; so it proved to be, indeed; the clock behind the partition made an effort and struck two. Mr. Golyadkin rushed behind the
partition.

He succeeded, somehow, though only after great exertions, in rousing Petrushka, and making him sit up in his bed. At that moment the
candle went out completely. About ten minutes passed before Mr.
Golyadkin succeeded in finding another candle and lighting it. In the
interval Petrushka had fallen asleep again.

"You scoundrel, you worthless fellow!" said Mr. Golyadkin, shaking
him up again. "Will you get up, will you wake?" After half an hour of
effort Mr. Golyadkin succeeded, however, in rousing his servant thoroughly, and dragging him out from behind the partition. Only then,
our hero remarked the fact that Petrushka was what is called dead-
drunk and could hardly stand on his legs.

"You good-for-nothing fellow!" cried Mr. Golyadkin; "you ruffian!
You'll be the death of me! Good heavens! whatever has he done with
the letter? Ach, my God! where is it? . . . And why did I write it? As
though there were any need for me to have written it! I went scribbling
away out of pride, like a noodle! I've got myself into this fix out of pride!
That is what dignity does for you, you rascal, that is dignity! . . . Come,
what have you done with the letter, you ruffian? To whom did you give
it?"

"I didn't give any one any letter; and I never had any letter . . . so
there!"

Mr. Golyadkin wrung his hands in despair.

"Listen, Pyotr . . . listen to me, listen to me. . . ."

"I am listening. . . ."

"Where have you been?—answer . . ."

"Where have I been. . . . I've been to see good people! What is it to
me!"

"Oh, Lord, have mercy on us! Where did you go, to begin with? Did
you go to the department? . . . Listen, Pyotr, perhaps you're drunk?"

"Me drunk! If I should be struck on the spot this minute, not a drop,
not a drop—so there. . . ."

"No, no, it's no matter your being drunk. . . . I only asked; it's all right
your being drunk; I don't mind, Petrushka, I don't mind. . . . Perhaps
it's only that you have forgotten, but you'll remember it all. Come, try
to remember—have you been to that clerk's, to Vahramyev's; have you
been to him or not?"

"I have not been, and there's no such clerk. Not if I were this
minute . . ."

"No, no, Pyotr! No, Petrushka, you know I don't mind. Why, you see I don't mind. . . . Come, what happened? To be sure, it's cold and damp in the street, and so a man has a drop, and it's no matter. I am not angry. I've been drinking myself to-day, my boy. . . . Come, think and try and remember, did you go to Vahramyev?"

"Well, then, now, this is how it was, it's the truth—I did go, if this very minute . . ."

"Come, that is right, Petrushka, that is quite right that you've been. You see I'm not angry. . . . Come, come," our hero went on, coaxing his servant more and more, patting him on the shoulder and smiling to him, "come, you had a little nip, you scoundrel. . . . You had two-penn'orth of something, I suppose? You're a sly rogue! Well, that's no matter; come, you see that I'm not angry. . . . I'm not angry, my boy, I'm not angry. . . ."

"No, I'm not a sly rogue, say what you like. . . . I only went to see some good friends. I'm not a rogue, and I never have been a rogue. . . ."

"Oh, no, no, Petrushka; listen, Petrushka, you know I'm not scolding when I called you a rogue. I said that in fun, I said it in a good sense. You see, Petrushka, it is sometimes a compliment to a man when you call him a rogue, a cunning fellow, that he's a sharp chap and would not let any one take him in. Some men like it. . . . Come, come, it doesn't matter! Come, tell me, Petrushka, without keeping anything back, openly, as to a friend . . . did you go to Vahramyev's, and did he give you the address?"

"He did give me the address, he did give me the address too. He's a nice gentleman! 'Your master,' says he, 'is a nice man,' says he, 'very nice man;' says he, 'I send my regards,' says he, 'to your master, thank him and say that I like him,' says he—'how I do respect your master,' says he. 'Because,' says he, 'your master, Petrushka,' says he, 'is a good man, and you,' says he, 'Petrushka, are a good man too. . . .'"

"Ah, mercy on us! But the address, the address! You Judas!" The last word Mr. Golyadkin uttered almost in a whisper.

"And the address . . . he did give the address too."

"He did? Well, where does Golyadkin, the clerk Golyadkin, the titular councillor, live?"

"'Why,' says he, 'Golyadkin will be now at Shestilavotchny Street. When you get into Shestilavotchny Street take the stairs on the right and it's the fourth floor. And there,' says he, 'you'll find Golyadkin. . . .'"

"You scoundrel!" our hero cried, out of patience at last. "You're a ruffian! Why, that's my address; why, you are talking about me. But there's another Golyadkin; I'm talking of the other one, you scoundrel!"

"Well, that's as you please! What is it to me? Have it your own way. . . ."

"And the letter, the letter? . . . "

"What letter? There wasn't any letter, and I didn't see any letter."

"But what have you done with it, you rascal?"

"I delivered the letter, I delivered it. He sent his regards. 'Thank you,' says he, 'your master's a nice man,' says he. 'Give my regards,' says he, 'to your master. . . .'"

"But who said that? Was it Golyadkin said it?"

Petrushka said nothing for a moment, and then, with a broad grin, he stared straight into his master's face. . . ."

"Listen, you scoundrel!" began Mr. Golyadkin, breathless, beside himself with fury; "listen, you rascal, what have you done to me? Tell me what you've done to me! You've destroyed me, you villain, you've cut the head off my shoulders, you Judas!"

"Well, have it your own way! I don't care," said Petrushka in a resolute voice, retreating behind the screen.

"Come here, come here, you ruffian. . . ."

"I'm not coming to you now, I'm not coming at all. What do I care, I'm going to good folks. . . . Good folks live honestly, good folks live without falsity, and they never have doubles. . . ."

Mr. Golyadkin's hands and feet went icy cold, his breath failed him. . . .

"Yes," Petrushka went on, "they never have doubles. God doesn't afflict honest folk. . . ."

"You worthless fellow, you are drunk! Go to sleep now, you ruffian! And to-morrow you'll catch it," Mr. Golyadkin added in a voice hardly audible. As for Petrushka, he muttered something more; then he could be heard getting into bed, making the bed creak. After a prolonged yawn, he stretched; and at last began snoring, and slept the sleep of the just, as they say. Mr. Golyadkin was more dead than alive. Petrushka's behaviour, his very strange hints, which were yet so remote that it was useless to be angry at them, especially as they were uttered by a drunken man, and, in short, the sinister turn taken by the affair altogether, all this shook Mr. Golyadkin to the depths of his being.

"And what possessed me to go for him in the middle of the night?" said our hero, trembling all over from a sickly sensation. "What the devil made me have anything to do with a drunken man! What could I expect from a drunken man? Whatever he says is a lie. But what was he hinting at, the ruffian? Lord, have mercy on us! And why did I write all that letter? I'm my own enemy, I'm my own murderer! As if I couldn't hold my tongue? I had to go scribbling nonsense! And what now! You are going to ruin, you are like an old rag, and yet you worry about your pride; you say, 'my honour is wounded,' you must stick up for your honour! My own murderer, that is what I am!"

Thus spoke Mr. Golyadkin and hardly dared to stir for terror. At last his eyes fastened upon an object which excited his interest to the utmost. In terror lest the object that caught his attention should prove to be an illusion, a deception of his fancy, he stretched out his hand to it with hope, with dread, with indescribable curiosity. . . . No, it was not a deception! Not a delusion! It was a letter, really a letter, undoubtedly a letter, and addressed to him. Mr. Golyadkin took the letter from the table. His heart beat terribly.

"No doubt that scoundrel brought it," he thought, "put it there, and then forgot it; no doubt that is how it happened: no doubt that is just how it happened. . . ."

The letter was from Vahramyev, a young fellow-clerk who had once been his friend. "I had a presentiment of this, though," thought our hero, "and I had a presentiment of all that there will be in the letter. . . ."

The letter was as follows —

"Dear Sir Yakov Petrovitch!
    "Your servant is drunk, and there is no getting any sense out of him. For that reason I prefer to reply by letter. I hasten to inform you that the commission you've entrusted to me — that is, to deliver a letter to a certain person you know, I agree to carry out carefully and exactly. That person, who is very well known to you and who has taken the place of a friend to me, whose name I will refrain from mentioning (because I do not wish unnecessarily to blacken the reputation of a perfectly innocent man), lodges with us at Karolina Ivanovna's, in the room in which, when you were among us, the infantry officer from Tambov used to be. That person, however, is always to be found in the company of honest and true-hearted persons, which is more than one can say for some people. I intend from this day to break off all connection with you; it's impossible for us to remain on friendly terms and to keep up the appearance of comradeship congruous with them. And, therefore, I beg you, my dear sir, immediately on the receipt of this candid letter from me, to send me the two roubles you owe me for the razor of foreign make which I sold you seven months ago, if you will kindly remember, when you were still living with us in the lodgings of Karolina Ivanovna, a lady whom I respect from the bottom of my heart. I am

acting in this way because you, from the accounts I hear from sensible persons, have lost your dignity and reputation and have become a source of danger to the morals of the innocent and uncontaminated. For some persons are not straightforward, their words are full of falsity and their show of good intentions is suspicious. People can always be found capable of insulting Karolina Ivanovna, who is always irreproachable in her conduct, and an honest woman, and, what's more, a maiden lady, though no longer young—though, on the other hand, of a good foreign family—and this fact I've been asked to mention in this letter by several persons, and I speak also for myself. In any case you will learn all in due time, if you haven't learnt it yet, though you've made yourself notorious from one end of the town to the other, according to the accounts I hear from sensible people, and consequently might well have received intelligence relating to you, my dear sir, in many places. In conclusion, I beg to inform you, my dear sir, that a certain person you know, whose name I will not mention here, for certain honourable reasons, is highly respected by right-thinking people, and is, moreover, of lively and agreeable disposition, and is equally successful in the service and in the society of persons of common sense, is true in word and in friendship, and does not insult behind their back those with whom he is on friendly terms to their face.

"In any case, I remain

"Your obedient servant,

"N. Vahramyev."

"P.S. You had better dismiss your man: he is a drunkard and probably gives you a great deal of trouble; you had better engage Yevstafy, who used to be in service here, and is now out of a place. Your present servant is not only a drunkard, but, what's more, he's a thief, for only last week he sold a pound of lump sugar to Karolina Ivanovna at less than cost price, which, in my opinion, he could not have done otherwise than by robbing you in a very sly way, little by little, at different times. I write this to you for your own good, although some people can do nothing but insult and deceive everybody, especially persons of honesty and good nature; what is more, they slander them behind their back and misrepresent them, simply from envy, and because they can't call themselves the same.

"V."

After reading Vahramyev's letter our hero remained for a long time sitting motionless on his sofa. A new light seemed breaking through the obscure and baffling fog which had surrounded him for the last two days. Our hero seemed to reach a partial understanding. . . . He tried to get up from the sofa to take a turn about the room, to rouse himself, to collect his scattered ideas, to fix them upon a certain subject and then to set himself to rights a little, to think over his position thoroughly. But as soon as he tried to stand up he fell back again at once, weak and helpless. "Yes, of course, I had a presentiment of all that; how he writes though, and what is the real meaning of his words. Supposing I do understand the meaning; but what is it leading to? He should have said straight out: this and that is wanted, and I would have done it. Things have taken such a turn, things have come to such an unpleasant pass! Oh, if only to-morrow would make haste and come, and I could make haste and get to work! I know now what to do. I shall say this and that, I shall agree with his arguments, I won't sell my honour, but . . . maybe; but he, that person we know of, that disagreeable person, how does he come to be mixed up in it? And why has he turned up here? Oh, if to-morrow would make haste and come! They'll slander me before then, they are intriguing, they are working to spite me! The great thing is not to lose time, and now, for instance, to write a letter, and to say this and that and that I agree to this and that. And as soon as it is daylight to-morrow send it off, before he can do anything . . . and so checkmate them, get in before them, the darlings. . . . They will ruin me by their slanders, and that's the fact of the matter!"

Mr. Golyadkin drew the paper to him, took up a pen and wrote the following missive in answer to the secretary's letter—

"Dear Sir Nestor Ignatyevitch!

"With amazement mingled with heartfelt distress I have perused your insulting letter to me, for I see clearly that you are referring to me when you speak of certain discreditable persons and false friends. I see with genuine sorrow how rapidly the calumny has spread and how deeply it has taken root, to the detriment of my prosperity, my honour and my good name. And this is the more distressing and mortifying that even honest people of a genuinely noble way of thinking and, what is even more important, of straightforward and open dispositions, abandon the interests of honourable men and with all the qualities of their hearts attach themselves to the pernicious corruption, which in our difficult and immoral age has unhappily increased and multiplied so greatly and so disloyally. In conclusion, I will say that the debt of two roubles of which you remind me I regard as a sacred duty to return to you in its entirety.

"As for your hints concerning a certain person of the female sex, concerning the intentions, calculations and various designs of that person,

I can only tell you, sir, that I have but a very dim and obscure under-standing of those insinuations. Permit me, sir, to preserve my hon-ourable way of thinking and my good name undefiled, in any case. I am ready to stoop to an explanation in person, preferring a personal inter-view to a written explanation as more secure, and I am, moreover, ready to enter into conciliatory proposals on mutual terms, of course. To that end I beg you, my dear sir, to convey to that person my readiness for a personal arrangement and, what is more, to beg her to fix the time and place of the interview. It grieved me, sir, to read your hints of my hav-ing insulted you, having been treacherous to our original friendship and having spoken ill of you. I ascribe this misunderstanding to the abominable calumny, envy and ill-will of those whom I may justly stig-matize as my bitterest foes. But I suppose they do not know that inno-cence is strong through its very innocence, that the shamelessness, the insolence and the revolting familiarity of some persons, sooner or later gains the stigma of universal contempt; and that such persons come to ruin through nothing but their own worthlessness and the corruption of their own hearts. In conclusion, I beg you, sir, to convey to those per-sons that their strange pretensions and their dishonourable and fantas-tic desire to squeeze others out of the position which those others occu-py, by their very existence in this world, and to take their place, are deserving of contempt, amazement, compassion and, what is more, the madhouse; moreover, such efforts are severely prohibited by law, which in my opinion is perfectly just, for every one ought to be satisfied with his own position. Every one has his fixed position, and if this is a joke it is a joke in very bad taste. I will say more: it is utterly immoral, for, I make bold to assure you, sir, my own views which I have expounded above, in regard to keeping *one's own place*, are purely moral.

"In any case I have the honour to remain,

"Your humble servant,

"Y. Golyadkin."

CHAPTER X

Altogether, we may say, the adventures of the previous day had thor-oughly unnerved Mr. Golyadkin. Our hero passed a very bad night; that is, he did not get thoroughly off to sleep for five minutes: as though some practical joker had scattered bristles in his bed. He spent the whole night in a sort of half-sleeping state, tossing from side to side, from right to left, moaning and groaning, dozing off for a moment, waking up again a minute later, and all was accompanied by a strange misery, vague memories, hideous visions—in fact, everything disagreeable that can be imagined. . . .

At one moment the figure of Andrey Filippovitch appeared before him in a strange, mysterious half-light. It was a frigid, wrathful figure, with a cold, harsh eye and with stiffly polite words of blame on its lips . . . and as soon as Mr. Golyadkin began going up to Andrey Filippovitch to defend himself in some way and to prove to him that he was not at all such as his enemies represented him, that he was like this and like that, that he even possessed innate virtues of his own, superior to the average—at once a person only too well known for his discreditable behaviour appeared on the scene, and by some most revolting means instantly frustrated poor Mr. Golyadkin's efforts, on the spot, almost before the latter's eyes, blackened his reputation, trampled his dignity in the mud, and then immediately took possession of his place in the service and in society.

At another time Mr. Golyadkin's head felt sore from some sort of slight blow of late conferred and humbly accepted, received either in the course of daily life or somehow in the performance of his duty, against which blow it was difficult to protest. . . . And while Mr. Golyadkin was racking his brains over the question why it was so difficult to protest even against such a blow, this idea of a blow gradually melted away into a different form—into the form of some familiar, trifling, or rather important piece of nastiness which he had seen, heard, or even himself committed—and frequently committed, indeed, and not on nasty grounds, not from any nasty impulse, even, but just because it happened—sometimes, for instance, out of delicacy, another time owing to his absolute defencelessness—in fact, because . . . because, in fact, Mr. Golyadkin knew perfectly well *because of what!* At this point Mr. Golyadkin blushed in his sleep, and, smothering his blushes, muttered to himself that in this case he ought to be able to show the strength of his character, he ought to be able to show in this case the remarkable strength of his character, and then wound up by asking himself, "What, after all, is strength of character? Why understand it now? . . ."

But what irritated and enraged Mr. Golyadkin most of all was that invariably, at such a moment, a person well known for his undignified burlesque behaviour turned up uninvited, and, regardless of the fact that the matter was apparently settled, he, too, would begin muttering, with an unseemly little smile "What's the use of strength of character! How could you and I, Yakov Petrovitch, have strength of character? . . ."

Then Mr. Golyadkin would dream that he was in the company of a number of persons distinguished for their wit and good breeding; that he, Mr. Golyadkin, too, was conspicuous for his wit and politeness, that everybody liked him, even some of his enemies who were present began to like him, which was very agreeable to Mr. Golyadkin; that every one gave him precedence, and that at last Mr. Golyadkin himself, with gratification, overheard the host, drawing one of the guests aside, speak in his, Mr. Golyadkin's, praise . . . and all of a sudden, apropos of nothing, there appeared again a person, notorious for his treachery and brutal impulses, in the form of Mr. Golyadkin junior, and on the spot, at once, by his very appearance on the scene, Mr. Golyadkin junior destroyed the whole triumph and glory of Mr. Golyadkin senior, eclipsed Mr. Golyadkin senior, trampled him in the mud, and, at last, proved clearly that Golyadkin senior—that is, the genuine one—was not the genuine one at all but the sham, and that he, Golyadkin junior, was the real one; that, in fact, Mr. Golyadkin senior was not at all what he appeared to be, but something very disgraceful, and that consequently he had no right to mix in the society of honourable and well-bred people. And all this was done so quickly that Mr. Golyadkin had not time to open his mouth before all of them were subjugated, body and soul, by the wicked, sham Mr. Golyadkin, and with profound contempt rejected him, the real and innocent Mr. Golyadkin. There was not one person left whose opinion the infamous Mr. Golyadkin would not have changed round. There was not left one person, even the most insignificant of the company, to whom the false and worthless Mr. Golyadkin would not make up in his blandest manner, upon whom he would not fawn in his own way, before whom he would not burn sweet and agreeable incense, so that the flattered person simply sniffed and sneezed till the tears came, in token of the intensest pleasure. And the worst of it was that all this was done in a flash: the swiftness of movement of the false and worthless Mr. Golyadkin was marvellous! He scarcely had time, for instance, to make up to one person and win his good graces— and before one could wink an eye he was at another. He stealthily fawns on another, drops a smile of benevolence, twirls on his short, round, though rather wooden-looking leg, and already he's at a third, and is cringing upon a third, he's making up to him in a friendly way; before one has time to open one's mouth, before one has time to feel surprised he's at a fourth, at the same manœuvres with him—it was horrible: sorcery and nothing else! And every one was pleased with him and everybody liked him, and every one was exalting him, and all were proclaiming in chorus that his politeness and sarcastic wit were infinitely superior to the politeness and sarcastic wit of the real Mr. Golyadkin and putting the real and innocent Mr. Golyadkin to shame thereby and rejecting the veritable Mr. Golyadkin, and shoving and pushing out the loyal Mr. Golyadkin, and showering blows on the man so well known for his love towards his fellow creatures! . . .

In misery, in terror and in fury, the cruelly treated Mr. Golyadkin ran out into the street and began trying to take a cab in order to drive straight to his Excellency's, or, at any rate, to Andrey Filippovitch's, but—horror! the cabman absolutely refused to take Mr. Golyadkin, saying, "We cannot drive two gentlemen exactly alike, sir; a good man tries to live honestly, your honour, and never has a double." Overcome with shame, the unimpeachable, honest Mr. Golyadkin looked round and did, in fact, assure himself with his own eyes that the cabman and Petrushka, who had joined them, were all quite right, for the depraved Mr. Golyadkin was actually on the spot, beside him, close at hand, and with his characteristic nastiness was again, at this critical moment, certainly preparing to do something very unseemly, and quite out of keeping with that gentlemanliness of character which is usually acquired by good breeding— that gentlemanliness of which the loathsome Mr. Golyadkin the second was always boasting on every opportunity. Beside himself with shame and despair, the utterly ruined though perfectly just Mr. Golyadkin dashed headlong away, wherever fate might lead him; but with every step he took, with every thud of his foot on the granite of the pavement, there leapt up as though out of the earth a Mr. Golyadkin precisely the same, perfectly alike, and of a revolting depravity of heart. And all these precisely similar Golyadkins set to running after one another as soon as they appeared, and stretched in a long chain like a file of geese, hobbling after the real Mr. Golyadkin, so there was nowhere to escape from these duplicates—so that Mr. Golyadkin, who was in every way deserving of compassion, was breathless with terror; so that at last a terrible multitude of duplicates had sprung into being; so that the whole town was obstructed at last by duplicate Golyadkins, and the police officer, seeing such a breach of decorum, was obliged to seize all these duplicates by the collar and to put them into the watch-house, which happened to be beside him. . . . Numb and chill with horror, our hero woke up, and numb and chill with horror felt that his waking state was hardly more cheerful. . . . It was oppressive and harrowing. . . . He was overcome by such anguish that it seemed as though someone were gnawing at his heart.

At last Mr. Golyadkin could endure it no longer. "This shall not be!" he cried, resolutely sitting up in bed, and after this exclamation he felt fully awake.

It seemed as though it were rather late in the day. It was unusually light in the room. The sunshine filtered through the frozen panes and flooded the room with light, which surprised Mr. Golyadkin not a little and, so far as Mr. Golyadkin could remember, at least, there had scarcely ever been such exceptions in the course of the heavenly luminary before. Our hero had hardly time to wonder at this when he heard the clock buzzing behind the partition as though it was just on the point of striking. "Now," thought Mr. Golyadkin, and he prepared to listen with painful suspense. . . .

But to complete Mr. Golyadkin's astonishment, the clock whirred and only struck once.

"What does this mean?" cried our hero, finally leaping out of bed. And, unable to believe his ears, he rushed behind the screen just as he was. It actually was one o'clock. Mr. Golyadkin glanced at Petrushka's bed; but the room did not even smell of Petrushka: his bed had long been made and left, his boots were nowhere to be seen either—an unmistakable sign that Petrushka was not in the house. Mr. Golyadkin rushed to the door: the door was locked. "But where is he, where is Petrushka?" he went on in a whisper, conscious of intense excitement and feeling a perceptible tremor run all over him . . . Suddenly a thought floated into his mind . . . Mr. Golyadkin rushed to the table, looked all over it, felt all round—yes, it was true, his letter of the night before to Vahramyev was not there. Petrushka was nowhere behind the screen either, the clock had just struck one, and some new points were evident to him in Vahramyev's letter, points that were obscure at first sight though now they were fully explained. Petrushka had evidently been bribed at last! "Yes, yes, that was so!"

"So this was how the chief plot was hatched!" cried Mr. Golyadkin, slapping himself on the forehead, opening his eyes wider and wider; "so in that filthy German woman's den the whole power of evil lies hidden now! So she was only making a strategic diversion in directing me to the Ismailovsky Bridge--she was putting me off the scent, confusing me (the worthless witch), and in that way laying her mines! Yes, that is so! If one only looks at the thing from that point of view, all of this is bound to be so, and the scoundrel's appearance on the scene is fully explained: it's all part and parcel of the same thing. They've kept him in reserve a long while, they had him in readiness for the evil day. This is how it has all turned out! This is what it has come to. But there, never mind. No time has been lost so far."

At this point Mr. Golyadkin recollected with horror that it was past one in the afternoon. "What if they have succeeded by now? . . ." He uttered a moan. . . . "But, no, they are lying, they've not had time—we shall see. . . ."

He dressed after a fashion, seized paper and a pen, and scribbled the following missive—

"Dear Sir Yakov Petrovitch!

"Either you or I, but both together is out of the question! And so I must inform you that your strange, absurd, and at the same time impossible desire to appear to be my twin and give yourself out as such serves no other purpose than to bring about your complete disgrace and discomfiture. And so I beg you, for the sake of your own advantage, to step aside and make way for really honourable men of loyal aims. In the opposite case I am ready to determine upon extreme measures. I lay down my pen and await . . . However, I remain ready to oblige or to meet you with pistols.

"Y. GOLYADKIN."

Our hero rubbed his hands energetically when he had finished the letter. Then, pulling on his greatcoat and putting on his hat, he unlocked his flat with a spare key and set off for the department. He reached the office but could not make up his mind to go in—it was by now too late. It was half-past two by Mr. Golyadkin's watch. All at once a circumstance of apparently little importance settled some doubts in Mr. Golyadkin's mind: a flushed and breathless figure suddenly made its appearance from behind the screen of the department building and with a stealthy movement like a rat he darted up the steps and into the entry. It was a copying clerk called Ostafyev, a man Mr. Golyadkin knew very well, who was rather useful and ready to do anything for a trifle. Knowing Ostafyev's weak spot and surmising that after his brief, unavoidable absence he would probably be greedier than ever for tips, our hero made up his mind not to be sparing of them, and immediately darted up the steps, and then into the entry after him, called to him and, with a mysterious air, drew him aside into a convenient corner behind a huge iron stove. And having led him there, our hero began questioning him.

"Well, my dear fellow, how are things going in there . . . you understand me? . . ."

"Yes, your honour, I wish you good health, your honour."

"All right, my good man, all right; but I'll reward you, my good fellow. Well, you see, how are things?"

"What is your honour asking?" At this point Ostafyev held his hand as though by accident before his open mouth.

"You see, my dear fellow, this is how it is . . . but don't you imagine . . . Come, is Andrey Filippovitch here? . . ."

"Yes, he is here."

"And are the clerks here?"

"Yes, sir, they are here as usual."

"And his Excellency too?"

"And his Excellency too." Here the man held his hand before his
open mouth again, and looked rather curiously and strangely at Mr.
Golyadkin, so at least our hero fancied.

"And there's nothing special there, my good man?"

"No, sir, certainly not, sir."

"So there's nothing concerning me, my friend. Is there nothing going
on there—that is, nothing more than . . . eh? nothing more, you understand, my friend?"

"No, sir, I've heard nothing so far, sir." Again the man put his hand
before his mouth and again looked rather strangely at Mr. Golyadkin.
The fact was, Mr. Golyadkin was trying to read Ostafyev's countenance,
trying to discover whether there was not something hidden in it. And,
in fact, he did look as though he were hiding something: Ostafyev
seemed to grow colder and more churlish, and did not enter into Mr.
Golyadkin's interests with the same sympathy as at the beginning of the
conversation. "He is to some extent justified," thought Mr. Golyadkin.
"After all, what am I to him? Perhaps he has already been bribed by the
other side, and that's why he has just been absent. But, here, I'll try
him. . . ." Mr. Golyadkin realized that the moment for kopecks had
arrived.

"Here, my dear fellow . . ."

"I'm feelingly grateful for your honour's kindness."

"I'll give you more than that."

"Yes, your honour."

"I'll give you some more directly, and when the business is over I'll
give you as much again. Do you understand?"

The clerk did not speak. He stood at attention and stared fixedly at
Mr. Golyadkin.

"Come, tell me now: have you heard nothing about me? . . ."

"I think, so far, I have not . . . so to say . . . nothing so far." Ostafyev,
like Mr. Golyadkin, spoke deliberately and preserved a mysterious air,
moving his eyebrows a little, looking at the ground, trying to fall into
the suitable tone, and, in fact, doing his very utmost to earn what had
been promised him, for what he had received already he reckoned as
already earned.

"And you know nothing?"

"So far, nothing, sir."

"Listen . . . you know . . . maybe you will know . . ."

"Later on, of course, maybe I shall know."

"It's a poor look out," thought our hero. "Listen: here's something more, my dear fellow."

"I am truly grateful to your honour."

"Was Vahramyev here yesterday? . . ."

"Yes, sir."

"And . . . somebody else? . . . Was he? . . . Try and remember, brother."

The man ransacked his memory for a moment, and could think of nothing appropriate.

"No, sir, there wasn't anybody else."

"H'm!" a silence followed.

"Listen, brother, here's some more; tell me all, every detail."

"Yes, sir," Ostafyev had by now become as soft as silk; which was just what Mr. Golyadkin needed.

"Explain to me now, my good man, what footing is he on?"

"All right, sir, a good one, sir," answered the man, gazing open-eyed at Mr. Golyadkin.

"How do you mean, all right?"

"Well, it's just like that, sir." Here Ostafyev twitched his eyebrows significantly. But he was utterly nonplussed and didn't know what more to say.

"It's a poor look out," thought Mr Golyadkin.

"And hasn't anything more happened . . . in there . . . about Vahramyev?"

"But everything is just as usual."

"Think a little."

"There is, they say . . ."

"Come, what?"

Ostafyev put his hand in front of his mouth.

"Wasn't there a letter . . . from here . . . to me?"

"Mihyeev the attendant went to Vahramyev's lodging, to their German landlady, so I'll go and ask him, if you like."

"Do me the favour, brother, for goodness' sake! . . . I only mean . . . you mustn't imagine anything, brother, I only mean . . . Yes, you question him, brother, find out whether they are not getting up something concerning me. Find out how he is acting. That is what I want; that is what you must find out, my dear fellow, and then I'll reward you, my good man. . . ."

"I will, your honour, and Ivan Semyonovitch sat in your place to-day, sir."

"Ivan Semyonovitch? Oh! really, you don't say so."

"Andrey Filippovitch told him to sit there."

"Re-al-ly! How did that happen? You must find out, brother; for God's sake find out, brother; find it all out—and I'll reward you, my dear fellow; that's what I want to know . . . and don't you imagine anything, brother. . . ."

"Just so, sir, just so; I'll go at once. And aren't you going in to-day, sir?"

"No, my friend; I only looked round, I only looked round, you know. I only came to have a look round, my friend, and I'll reward you afterwards, my friend."

"Yes, sir." The man ran rapidly and eagerly up the stairs and Mr. Golyadkin was left alone.

"It's a poor look out!" he thought. "Ech, it's a bad business, a bad business! Ech! things are in a bad way with us now! What does it all mean? What did that drunkard's insinuations mean, for instance, and whose trickery was it? Ah! I know now whose it was. And what a thing this is. No doubt they found out and made him sit there. . . . But, after all, did they sit him there? It was Andrey Filippovitch sat him there, he sat Ivan Semyonovitch there himself; why did he make him sit there and with what object? Probably they found out. . . . That is Vahramyev's work— that is, not Vahramyev, he is as stupid as an ashen post, Vahramyev is, and they are all at work on his behalf, and they egged that scoundrel on to come here for the same purpose, and the German woman brought up her grievance, the one-eyed hussy. I always suspected that this intrigue was not without an object and that in all this old-womanish gossip there must be something, and I said as much to Krestyan Ivanovitch, telling him they'd sworn to cut a man's throat—in a moral sense, of course— and they pounced upon Karolina Ivanovna. Yes, there are master hands at work in this, one can see! Yes, sir, there are master hands at work here, and not Vahramyev's. I've said already that Vahramyev is stupid, but . . . I know who it is behind it all, it's that rascal, that impostor! It's only that he relies upon, which is partly proved by his successes in the best society. And it would certainly be desirable to know on what footing he stands now. What is he now among them? Only, why have they taken Ivan Semyonovitch? What the devil do they want with Ivan Semyonovitch? Could not they have found any one else? Though it would come to the same thing whoever it had been, and the only thing I know is that I have suspected Ivan Semyonovitch for a long time past. I noticed long ago what a nasty, horrid old man he was—they say he lends money

and takes interest like any Jew. To be sure, the bear's the leading spirit in
the whole affair. One can detect the bear in the whole affair. It began in
this way. It began at the Ismailovsky Bridge; that's how it began . . ."

At this point Mr. Golyadkin frowned, as though he had taken a bite
out of a lemon, probably remembering something very unpleasant.

"But, there, it doesn't matter," he thought. "I keep harping on my
own troubles. What will Ostafyev find out? Most likely he is staying on
or has been delayed somehow. It is a good thing, in a sense, that I am
intriguing like this, and am laying mines on my side too. I've only to
give Ostafyev ten kopecks and he's . . . so to speak, on my side. Only the
point is, is he really on my side? Perhaps they've got him on their side
too . . . and they are carrying on an intrigue by means of him on their
side too. He looks a ruffian, the rascal, a regular ruffian; he's hiding
something, the rogue. 'No, nothing,' says he, 'and I am deeply grateful
to your honour,' says he. You ruffian, you!"

He heard a noise . . . Mr. Golyadkin shrank up and skipped behind
the stove. Some one came down stairs and went out into the street.
"Who could that be going away now?" our hero thought to himself. A
minute later footsteps were audible again. . . . At this point Mr. Golyadkin could not resist poking the very tip of his nose out beyond his corner—he poked it out and instantly withdrew it again, as though some
one had pricked it with a pin. This time some one he knew well was
coming—that is the scoundrel, the intriguer and the reprobate—he was
approaching with his usual mean, tripping little step, prancing and
shuffling with his feet as though he were going to kick some one.

"The rascal," said our hero to himself.

Mr. Golyadkin could not, however, help observing that the rascal
had under his arm a huge green portfolio belonging to his Excellency.

"He's on a special commission again," thought Mr. Golyadkin, flushing crimson and shrinking into himself more than ever from vexation.

As soon as Mr. Golyadkin junior had slipped past Mr. Golyadkin
senior without observing him in the least, footsteps were heard for the
third time, and this time Mr. Golyadkin guessed that these were
Ostafyev's. It was, in fact, the sleek figure of a copying clerk, Pisarenko
by name. This surprised Mr. Golyadkin. Why had he mixed up other
people in their secret? our hero wondered. What barbarians! nothing is
sacred to them! "Well, my friend?" he brought out, addressing Pisarenko: "who sent you, my friend? . . ."

"I've come about your business. There's no news so far from any one.
But should there be any we'll let you know."

"And Ostafyev?"

"It was quite impossible for him to come, your honour. His Excellency has walked through the room twice, and I've no time to stay."

"Thank you, my good man, thank you . . . only, tell me . . ."

"Upon my word, sir, I can't stay. . . . They are asking for us every minute . . . but if your honour will stay here, we'll let you know if anything happens concerning your little affair."

"No, my friend, you just tell me . . ."

"Excuse me, I've no time to stay, sir," said Pisarenko, tearing himself away from Mr. Golyadkin, who had clutched him by the lapel of his coat. "I really can't. If your honour will stay here we'll let you know."

"In a minute, my good man, in a minute! In a minute, my good fellow! I tell you what, here's a letter; and I'll reward you, my good man."

"Yes, sir."

"Try and give it to Mr. Golyadkin my dear fellow."

"Golyadkin?"

"Yes, my man, to Mr. Golyadkin."

"Very good, sir; as soon as I get off I'll take it, and you stay here, meanwhile; no one will see you here. . . ."

"No, my good man, don't imagine . . . I'm not standing here to avoid being seen. But I'm not going to stay here now, my friend. . . . I'll be close here in the side street. There's a coffee-house near here; so I'll wait there, and if anything happens, you let me know about anything, you understand?"

"Very good, sir. Only let me go; I understand."

"And I'll reward you," Mr. Golyadkin called after Pisarenko, when he had at last released him. . . .

"The rogue seemed to be getting rather rude," our hero reflected as he stealthily emerged from behind the stove. "There's some other dodge here. That's clear. . . . At first it was one thing and another . . . he really was in a hurry, though; perhaps there's a great deal to do in the office. And his Excellency had been through the room twice. . . . How did that happen? . . . Ough! never mind! It may mean nothing, perhaps; but now we shall see. . . ."

At this point Mr. Golyadkin was about to open the door, intending to go out into the street, when suddenly, at that very instant, his Excellency's carriage dashed up to the door. Before Mr. Golyadkin had time to recover from the shock, the door of the carriage was opened from within and a gentleman jumped out. This gentleman was no other than Mr. Golyadkin junior, who had only gone out ten minutes before. Mr. Golyadkin senior remembered that the Director's flat was only a couple of paces away.

"He has been out on a special commission," our hero thought to himself.

Meanwhile, Mr. Golyadkin junior took out of the carriage a thick green portfolio and other papers. Finally, giving some orders to the coachman, he opened the door, almost ran up against Mr. Golyadkin senior, purposely avoided noticing him, acting in this way expressly to annoy him, and mounted the office staircase at a rapid canter.

"It's a bad look out," thought Mr. Golyadkin. "This is what it has come to now! Oh, good Lord! look at him."

For half a minute our hero remained motionless. At last he made up his mind. Without pausing to think, though he was aware of a violent palpitation of the heart and a tremor in all his limbs, he ran up the stairs after his enemy.

"Here goes; what does it matter to me? I have nothing to do with the case," he thought, taking off his hat, his greatcoat and his goloshes in the entry.

When Mr. Golyadkin walked into his office, it was already getting dusk. Neither Andrey Filippovitch nor Anton Antonovitch were in the room. Both of them were in the Director's room, handing in reports. The Director, so it was rumoured, was in haste to report to a still higher Excellency. In consequence of this, and also because twilight was coming on, and the office hours were almost over, several of the clerks, especially the younger ones, were, at the moment when our hero entered, enjoying a period of inactivity; gathered together in groups, they were talking, arguing, and laughing, and some of the most youthful—that is, belonging to the lowest grades in the service, had got up a game of pitch-farthing in a corner, by a window. Knowing what was proper, and feeling at the moment a special need to conciliate and get on with them, Mr. Golyadkin immediately approached those with whom he used to get on best, in order to wish them good day, and so on. But his colleagues answered his greetings rather strangely. He was unpleasantly impressed by a certain coldness, even curtness, one might almost say severity in their manner. No one shook hands with him. Some simply said, "Good day" and walked away; others barely nodded; one simply turned away and pretended not to notice him; at last some of them—and what mortified Mr. Golyadkin most of all, some of the youngsters of the lowest grades, mere lads who, as Mr. Golyadkin justly observed about them, were capable of nothing but hanging about and playing pitch-farthing at every opportunity—little by little collected round Mr. Golyadkin, formed a group round him and almost barred his way. They all looked at him with a sort of insulting curiosity.

It was a bad sign. Mr. Golyadkin felt this, and very judiciously decided not to notice it. Suddenly a quite unexpected event completely finished him off, as they say, and utterly crushed him.

At the moment most trying to Mr. Golyadkin senior, suddenly, as though by design, there appeared in the group of fellow clerks surrounding him the figure of Mr. Golyadkin junior, gay as ever, smiling a little smile as ever, nimble, too, as ever; in short, mischievous, skipping and tripping, chuckling and fawning, with sprightly tongue and sprightly toe, as always, precisely as he had been the day before at a very unpleasant moment for Mr. Golyadkin senior, for instance.

Grinning, tripping and turning with a smile that seemed to say "good evening," to every one, he squeezed his way into the group of clerks, shaking hands with one, slapping another on the shoulder, putting his arm round another, explaining to a fourth how he had come to be employed by his Excellency, where he had been, what he had done, what he had brought with him; to the fifth, probably his most intimate friend, he gave a resounding kiss—in fact, everything happened as it had in Mr. Golyadkin's dream. When he had skipped about to his heart's content, polished them all off in his usual way, disposed them all in his favour, whether he needed them or not, when he had lavished his blandishments to the delectation of all the clerks, Mr. Golyadkin junior suddenly, and most likely by mistake, for he had not yet had time to notice his senior, held out his hand to Mr. Golyadkin senior also. Probably also by mistake—though he had had time to observe the dishonourable Mr. Golyadkin junior thoroughly, our hero at once eagerly seized the hand so unexpectedly held out to him and pressed it in the warmest and friendliest way, pressed it with a strange, quite unexpected, inner feeling, with a tearful emotion. Whether our hero was misled by the first movement of his worthless foe, or was taken unawares, or, without recognizing it, felt at the bottom of his heart how defenceless he was—it is difficult to say. The fact remains that Mr. Golyadkin senior, apparently knowing what he was doing, of his own free will, before witnesses, solemnly shook hands with him whom he called his mortal foe. But what was the amazement, the stupefaction and fury, what was the horror and the shame of Mr. Golyadkin senior, when his enemy and mortal foe, the dishonourable Mr. Golyadkin junior, noticing the mistake of that persecuted, innocent, perfidiously deceived man, without a trace of shame, of feeling, of compassion or of conscience, pulled his hand away

with insufferable rudeness and insolence. What was worse, he shook the
hand as though it had been polluted with something horrid; what is
more, he spat aside with disgust, accompanying this with a most insulting gesture; worse still, he drew out his handkerchief and, in the most
unseemly way, wiped all the fingers that had rested for one moment in
the hand of Mr. Golyadkin senior. While he did this Mr. Golyadkin
junior looked about him in his characteristic horrid way, took care that
every one should see what he was doing, glanced into people's eyes and
evidently tried to insinuate to every one everything that was most
unpleasant in regard to Mr. Golyadkin senior. Mr. Golyadkin junior's
revolting behaviour seemed to arouse general indignation among the
clerks that surrounded them; even the frivolous youngsters showed their
displeasure. A murmur of protest rose on all sides. Mr. Golyadkin could
not but discern the general feeling; but suddenly—an appropriate witti-
cism that bubbled from the lips of Mr. Golyadkin junior shattered, annihilated our hero's last hopes, and inclined the balance again in favour
of his deadly and undeserving foe.

"He's our Russian Faublas, gentlemen; allow me to introduce the
youthful Faublas," piped Mr. Golyadkin junior, with his characteristic
insolence, pirouetting and threading his way among the clerks, and
directing their attention to the petrified though genuine Mr. Golyadkin. "Let us kiss each other, darling," he went on with insufferable
familiarity, addressing the man he had so treacherously insulted. Mr.
Golyadkin junior's unworthy jest seemed to touch a responsive chord,
for it contained an artful allusion to an incident with which all were
apparently familiar. Our hero was painfully conscious of the hand of his
enemies. But he had made up his mind by now. With glowing eyes,
with pale face, with a fixed smile he tore himself somehow out of the
crowd and with uneven, hurried steps made straight for his Excellency's
private room. In the room next to the last he was met by Andrey Filippovitch, who had only just come out from seeing his Excellency, and
although there were present in this room at the moment a good number of persons of whom Mr. Golyadkin knew nothing, yet our hero did
not care to take such a fact into consideration. Boldly, resolutely, directly, almost wondering at himself and inwardly admiring his own
courage, without loss of time he accosted Andrey Filippovitch, who was
a good deal surprised by this unexpected attack.

"Ah! . . . What is it . . . what do you want?" asked the head of the divi-
sion, not hearing Mr. Golyadkin's hesitating words.

"Andrey Filippovitch, may . . . might I, Andrey Filippovitch, may I have a conversation with his Excellency at once and in private?" our hero said resolutely and distinctly, fixing the most determined glance on Andrey Filippovitch.

"What next! of course not." Andrey Filippovitch scanned Mr. Golyadkin from head to foot.

"I say all this, Andrey Filippovitch, because I am surprised that no one here unmasks the impostor and scoundrel."

"Wha-a-at!"

"Scoundrel, Andrey Filippovitch!"

"Of whom are you pleased to speak in those terms?"

"Of a certain person, Andrey Filippovitch; I'm alluding, Andrey Filippovitch, to a certain person; I have the right . . . I imagine, Andrey Filippovitch, that the authorities would surely encourage such action," added Mr. Golyadkin, evidently hardly knowing what he was saying. "Andrey Filippovitch . . . but no doubt you see yourself, Andrey Filippovitch, that this honourable action is a mark of my loyalty in every way—of my looking upon my superior as a father, Andrey Filippovitch; I as much as to say look upon my benevolent superior as a father and blindly trust my fate to him. It's as much as to say . . . you see . . ." At this point Mr. Golyadkin's voice trembled and two tears ran down his eyelashes.

As Andrey Filippovitch listened to Mr. Golyadkin he was so astonished that he could not help stepping back a couple of paces. Then he looked about him uneasily . . . It is difficult to say how the matter would have ended. But suddenly the door of his Excellency's room was opened, and he himself came out, accompanied by several officials. All the persons in his room following in a string. His Excellency called Andrey Filippovitch and walked beside him, beginning to discuss some business details. When all had set off and gone out of the room, Mr. Golyadkin woke up. Growing calmer, he took refuge under the wing of Anton Antonovitch, who came last in the procession and who, Mr. Golyadkin fancied, looked stern and anxious. "I've been talking nonsense, I've been making a mess of it again, but there, never mind," he thought.

"I hope, at least, that you, Anton Antonovitch, will consent to listen to me and to enter into my position," he said quietly, in a voice that still trembled a little. "Rejected by all, I appeal to you. I am still at a loss to understand what Andrey Filippovitch's words mean, Anton Antonovitch. Explain them to me if you can. . . ."

"Everything will be explained in due time," Anton Antonovitch replied sternly and emphatically, and as Mr. Golyadkin fancied with an air that gave him plainly to understand that Anton Antonovitch did not wish to continue the conversation. "You will soon know all about it. You will be officially informed about every thing to-day."

"What do you mean by officially informed, Anton Antonovitch? Why officially?" our hero asked timidly.

"It is not for you and me to discuss what our superiors decide upon, Yakov Petrovitch."

"Why our superiors, Anton Antonovitch?" said our hero, still more intimidated; "why our superiors? I don't see what reason there is to trouble our superiors in the matter, Anton Antonovitch . . . Perhaps you mean to say something about yesterday's doings, Anton Antonovitch?"

"Oh no, nothing to do with yesterday; there's something else amiss with you."

"What is there amiss, Anton Antonovitch? I believe, Anton Antonovitch, that I have done nothing amiss."

"Why, you were meaning to be sly with some one," Anton Antonovitch cut in sharply, completely flabbergasting Mr. Golyadkin.

Mr. Golyadkin started, and turned as white as a pocket-handkerchief.

"Of course, Anton Antonovitch," he said, in a voice hardly audible, "if one listens to the voice of calumny and hears one's enemies' tales, without heeding what the other side has to say in its defence, then, of course . . . then, of course, Anton Antonovitch, one must suffer innocently and for nothing."

"To be sure; but your unseemly conduct, in injuring the reputation of a virtuous young lady belonging to that benevolent, highly distinguished and well-known family who had befriended you . . ."

"What conduct do you mean, Anton Antonovitch?"

"What I say. Do you know anything about your praiseworthy conduct in regard to that other young lady who, though poor, is of honourable foreign extraction?"

"Allow me, Anton Antonovitch . . . if you would kindly listen to me, Anton Antonovitch . . ."

"And your treacherous behaviour and slander of another person, your charging another person with your own sins. Ah, what do you call that?"

"I did not send him away, Anton Antonovitch," said our hero, with a tremor; "and I've never instructed Petrushka, my man, to do anything of the sort . . . He has eaten my bread, Anton Antonovitch, he has taken advantage of my hospitality," our hero added expressively and with deep emotion, so much so that his chin twitched a little and tears were ready to start again.

"That is only your talk, that he has eaten your bread," answered Anton Antonovitch, somewhat offended, and there was a perfidious note in his voice which sent a pang to Mr. Golyadkin's heart.

"Allow me most humbly to ask you again, Anton Antonovitch, is his Excellency aware of all this business?"

"Upon my word, you must let me go now, though. I've no time for you now. . . . You'll know everything you need to know to-day."

"Allow me, for God's sake, one minute, Anton Antonovitch."

"Tell me afterwards . . ."

"No, Anton Antonovitch; I . . . you see, Anton Antonovitch . . . only listen . . . I am not one for freethinking, Anton Antonovitch; I shun free-thinking; I am quite ready for my part . . . and, indeed, I've given up that idea. . . ."

"Very good, very good. I've heard that already."

"No, you have not heard it, Anton Antonovitch. It is something else, Anton Antonovitch; it's a good thing, really, a good thing and pleasant to hear. . . . As I've explained to you, Anton Antonovitch, I admit that idea, that divine Providence has created two men exactly alike, and that a benevolent government, seeing the hand of Providence, provided a berth for two twins. That is a good thing, Anton Antonovitch. You see that it is a very good thing, Anton Antonovitch, and that I am very far from freethinking. I look upon my benevolent government as a father; I say 'yes,' by all means; you are benevolent authorities, and you, of course. . . . A young man must be in the service. . . . Stand up for me, Anton Antonovitch, take my part, Anton Antonovitch. . . . I am all right . . . Anton Antonovitch, for God's sake, one little word more . . . Anton Antonovitch. . . ."

But by now Anton Antonovitch was far away from Mr. Golyadkin. . . . Our hero was so bewildered and overcome by all that had happened and all that he had heard that he did not know where he was standing, what he had heard, what he had done, what was being done to him, and what was going to be done to him.

With imploring eyes he sought for Anton Antonovitch in the crowd of clerks, that he might justify himself further in his eyes and say something to him extremely high toned and very agreeable, and creditable to himself. . . . By degrees, however, a new light began to break upon our hero's bewildered mind, a new and awful light that revealed at once a whole perspective of hitherto unknown and utterly unsuspected circumstances. . . . At that moment somebody gave our bewildered hero a poke in the ribs. He looked around. Pisarenko was standing before him.

"A letter, your honour."

"Ah, you've been out already, then, my good man?"

"No, it was brought at ten o'clock this morning. Sergey Mihyeev, the attendant, brought it from Mr. Vahramyev's lodging."

"Very good, very good, and I'll reward you now, my dear fellow."

Saying this, Mr. Golyadkin thrust the letter in the side pocket of his uniform and buttoned up every button of it; then he looked round him, and to his surprise, found that he was by now in the hall of the department, in a group of clerks crowding at the outer door, for office hours were over. Mr. Golyadkin had not only failed till that moment to observe this circumstance, but had no notion how he suddenly came to be wearing his greatcoat and goloshes and to be holding his hat in his hand. All the clerks were standing motionless, in reverential expectation. The fact was that his Excellency was standing at the bottom of the stairs waiting for his carriage, which was for some reason late in arriving, and was carrying on a very interesting conversation with Andrey Filippovitch and two councillors. At a little distance from Andrey Filippovitch stood Anton Antonovitch and several other clerks, who were all smiles, seeing that his Excellency was graciously making a joke. The clerks who were crowded at the top of the stairs were smiling too, in expectation of his Excellency's laughing again. The only one who was not smiling was Fedosyevitch, the corpulent hall-porter, who stood stiffly at attention, holding the handle of the door, waiting impatiently for the daily gratification that fell to his share—that is, the task of flinging one half of the door wide open with a swing of his arm, and then, with a low bow, reverentially making way for his Excellency to pass. But the one who seemed to be more delighted than any and to feel the most satisfaction of all was the worthless and ungentlemanly enemy of Mr. Golyadkin. At that instant he positively forgot all the clerks, and even gave up tripping and pirouetting in his usual odious way; he even forgot to make up to anybody. He was all eyes and ears, he even doubled himself up strangely, no doubt in the strained effort to hear, and never took his eyes off his Excellency, and only from time to time his arms, legs and head twitched with faintly perceptible tremors that betrayed the secret emotions of his soul.

"Ah, isn't he in a state!" thought our hero; "he looks like a favourite, the rascal! I should like to know how it is that he deceives society of every class. He has neither brains nor character, neither education nor feeling; he's a lucky rogue! Mercy on us! How can a man, when you think of it, come and make friends with every one so quickly! And he'll get on, I swear the fellow will get on, the rogue will make his way—he's a lucky rascal! I should like to know, too, what he keeps whispering to

every one—what plots he is hatching with all these people, and what
secrets they are talking about? Lord, have mercy on us! If only I
could . . . get on with them a little too . . . say this and that and the other.
Hadn't I better ask him . . . tell him I won't do it again; say 'I'm in fault,
and a young man must serve nowadays, your Excellency'? I am not in
the least abashed by my obscure position—so there! I am not going to
protest in any way, either; I shall bear it all with meekness and patience,
so there! Is that the way to behave? . . . Though you'll never see through
him, though, the rascal; you can't reach him with anything you say; you
can't hammer reason into his head. . . . We'll make an effort, though. I
may happen to hit on a good moment, so I'll make an effort. . . ."

Feeling in his uneasiness, his misery and his bewilderment that he
couldn't leave things like this, that the critical moment had come, that
he must explain himself to some one, our hero began to move a little
towards the place where his worthless and undeserving enemy stood:
but at that very moment his Excellency's long-expected carriage rolled
up into the entrance, Fedosyevitch flung open the door and, bending
double, let his Excellency pass out. All the waiting clerks streamed out
towards the door, and for a moment separated Mr. Golyadkin senior
from Mr. Golyadkin junior.

"You shan't get away!" said our hero, forcing his way through the
crowd while he kept his eyes fixed on the man he wanted. At last the
crowd dispersed. Our hero felt he was free and flew in pursuit of his
enemy.

CHAPTER XI

MR. GOLYADKIN'S breath failed him; he flew as though on wings after
his rapidly retreating enemy. He was conscious of immense energy. Yet
in spite of this terrible energy he might confidently have said that at that
moment a humble gnat—had a gnat been able to exist in Petersburg at
that time of the year—could very easily have knocked him down. He
felt, too, that he was utterly weak again, that he was carried along by a
peculiar outside force, that it was not he himself who was running, but,
on the contrary, that his legs were giving way under him, and refused to
obey him. This all might turn out for the best, however.

"Whether it is for the best or not for the best," thought Mr. Golyadkin, almost breathless from running so quickly, "but that the game is

lost there cannot be the slightest doubt now; that I am utterly done for is certain, definite, signed and ratified."

In spite of all this our hero felt as though he had risen from the dead, as though he had withstood a battalion, as though he had won a victory when he succeeded in clutching the overcoat of his enemy, who had already raised one foot to get into the cab he had engaged.

"My dear sir! My dear sir!" he shouted to the infamous Mr. Golyadkin junior, holding him by the button. "My dear sir, I hope that you . . ."

"No, please do not hope for anything," Mr. Golyadkin's heartless enemy answered evasively, standing with one foot on the step of the cab and vainly waving the other leg in the air, in his efforts to get in, trying to preserve his equilibrium, and at the same time trying with all his might to wrench his coat away from Mr. Golyadkin senior, while the latter held on to it with all the strength that had been vouchsafed to him by nature.

"Yakov Petrovitch, only ten minutes . . ."

"Excuse me, I've no time . . ."

"You must admit, Yakov Petrovitch . . . please, Yakov Petrovitch. . . . For God's sake, Yakov Petrovitch . . . let us have it out—in a straightforward way . . . one little second, Yakov Petrovitch . . ."

"My dear fellow, I can't stay," answered Mr. Golyadkin's dishonourable enemy, with uncivil familiarity, disguised as good-natured heartiness; "another time, believe me, with my whole soul and all my heart; but now I really can't . . ."

"Scoundrel!" thought our hero. "Yakov Petrovitch," he cried miserably. "I have never been your enemy. Spiteful people have described me unjustly. . . . I am ready, on my side . . . Yakov Petrovitch, shall we go in here together, at once, Yakov Petrovitch? And with all my heart, as you have so justly expressed it just now, and in straightforward, honourable language, as you have expressed it just now—here into this coffee-house; there the facts will explain themselves: they will really, Yakov Petrovitch. Then everything will certainly explain itself. . . ."

"Into the coffee-house? Very good. I am not against it. Let us go into the coffee-house on one condition only, my dear, on one condition—that these things shall be cleared up. We will have it all out, darling," said Mr. Golyadkin junior, getting out of the cab and shamelessly slapping our hero on the shoulder; "You friend of my heart, for your sake, Yakov Petrovitch, I am ready to go by the back street (as you were pleased to observe so aptly on one occasion, Yakov Petrovitch). Why, what a rogue he is! Upon my word, he does just what he likes with one!"

Mr. Golyadkin's false friend went on, fawning upon him and cajoling him with a little smile. The coffee-house which the two Mr. Golyadkins entered stood some distance away from the main street and was at the moment quite empty. A rather stout German woman made her appearance behind the counter. Mr. Golyadkin and his unworthy enemy went into the second room, where a puffy-looking boy with a closely shaven head was busy with a bundle of chips at the stove, trying to revive the smouldering fire. At Mr. Golyadkin junior's request chocolate was served.

"And a sweet little lady-tart," said Mr. Golyadkin junior, with a sly wink at Mr. Golyadkin senior.

Our hero blushed and was silent.

"Oh, yes, I forgot, I beg your pardon. I know your taste. We are sweet on charming little Germans, sir; you and I are sweet on charming and agreeable little Germans, aren't we, you upright soul? We take their lodgings, we seduce their morals, they win our hearts with their beer-soup and their milksoup, and we give them notes of different sorts, that's what we do, you Faublas, you deceiver!" All this Mr. Golyadkin junior said, making an unworthy though villainously artful allusion to a certain personage of the female sex, while he fawned upon our hero, smiled at him with an amiable air, with a deceitful show of being delighted with him and pleased to have met him. Seeing that Mr. Golyadkin senior was by no means so stupid and deficient in breeding and the manners of good society as to believe in him, the infamous man resolved to change his tactics and to make a more open attack upon him. After uttering his disgusting speech, the false Mr. Golyadkin ended by slapping the real and substantial Mr. Golyadkin on the shoulder, with a revolting effrontery and familiarity. Not content with that, he began playing pranks utterly unfit for well-bred society; he took it into his head to repeat his old, nauseous trick—that is, regardless of the resistance and faint cries of the indignant Mr. Golyadkin senior, he pinched the latter on the cheek. At the spectacle of such depravity our hero boiled within, but was silent . . . only for the time, however.

"That is the talk of my enemies," he answered at last, in a trembling voice, prudently restraining himself. At the same time our hero looked round uneasily towards the door. The fact was that Mr. Golyadkin junior seemed in excellent spirits, and ready for all sorts of little jokes, unseemly in a public place, and, speaking generally, not permissible by the laws of good manners, especially in well-bred society.

"Oh, well, in that case, as you please," Mr. Golyadkin junior gravely responded to our hero's thought, setting down upon the table the empty cup which he had gulped down with unseemly greed. "Well, there's no need for me to stay long with you, however. . . . Well, how are you getting on now, Yakov Petrovitch?"

"There's only one thing I can tell you, Yakov Petrovitch," our hero answered, with sangfroid and dignity; "I've never been your enemy."

"H'm. . . . Oh, what about Petrushka? Petrushka is his name, I fancy? Yes, it is Petrushka! Well, how is he? Well? The same as ever?"

"He's the same as ever, too, Yakov Petrovitch," answered Mr. Golyadkin senior, somewhat amazed. "I don't know, Yakov Petrovitch . . . from my standpoint . . . from a candid, honourable standpoint, Yakov Petrovitch, you must admit, Yakov Petrovitch. . . ."

"Yes, but you know yourself, Yakov Petrovitch," Mr. Golyadkin junior answered in a soft and expressive voice, so posing falsely as a sorrowful man overcome with remorse and deserving compassion. "You know yourself we live in difficult times. . . . I appeal to you, Yakov Petrovitch; you are an intelligent man and your reflections are just," Mr. Golyadkin junior said in conclusion, flattering Mr. Golyadkin senior in an abject way. "Life is not a game, you know yourself, Yakov Petrovitch," Mr. Golyadkin junior added, with vast significance, assuming the character of a clever and learned man, who is capable of passing judgments on lofty subjects.

"For my part, Yakov Petrovitch," our hero answered warmly, "for my part, scorning to be roundabout and speaking boldly and openly, using straightforward, honourable language and putting the whole matter on an honourable basis, I tell you I can openly and honourably assert, Yakov Petrovitch, that I am absolutely pure, and that, you know it yourself, Yakov Petrovitch, the error is mutual—it may all be the world's judgment, the opinion of the slavish crowd. . . . I speak openly, Yakov Petrovitch, everything is possible. I will say, too, Yakov Petrovitch, if you judge it in this way, if you look at the matter from a lofty, noble point of view, then I will boldly say, without false shame I will say, Yakov Petrovitch, it will positively be a pleasure to me to discover that I have been in error, it will positively be a pleasure to me to recognize it. You know yourself you are an intelligent man and, what is more, you are a gentleman. Without shame, without false shame, I am ready to recognize it," he wound up with dignity and nobility.

"It is the decree of destiny, Yakov Petrovitch . . . but let us drop all this," said Mr. Golyadkin junior. "Let us rather use the brief moment of our meeting for a more pleasant and profitable conversation, as is only suitable between two colleagues in the service. . . . Really, I have not succeeded in saying two words to you all this time. . . . I am not to blame for that, Yakov Petrovitch. . . ."

"Nor I," answered our hero warmly, "nor I, either! My heart tells me, Yakov Petrovitch, that I'm not to blame in all this matter. Let us blame fate for all this, Yakov Petrovitch," added Mr. Golyadkin senior, in a quick, conciliatory tone of voice. His voice began little by little to soften and to quaver.

"Well! How are you in health?" said the sinner in a sweet voice.

"I have a little cough," answered our hero, even more sweetly.

"Take care of yourself. There is so much illness going about, you may easily get quinsy; for my part I confess I've begun to wrap myself up in flannel."

"One may, indeed, Yakov Petrovitch, very easily get quinsy," our hero pronounced after a brief silence; "Yakov Petrovitch, I see that I have made a mistake, I remember with softened feelings those happy moments which we were so fortunate as to spend together, under my poor, though I venture to say, hospitable roof . . ."

"In your letter, however, you wrote something very different," said Mr. Golyadkin junior reproachfully, speaking on this occasion— though only on this occasion—quite justly.

"Yakov Petrovitch, I was in error. . . . I see clearly now that I was in error in my unhappy letter too. Yakov Petrovitch, I am ashamed to look at you, Yakov Petrovitch, you wouldn't believe. . . . Give me that letter that I may tear it to pieces before your eyes, Yakov Petrovitch, and if that is utterly impossible I entreat you to read it the other way before—precisely the other way before—that is, expressly with a friendly intention, giving the opposite sense to the whole letter. I was in error. Forgive me, Yakov Petrovitch, I was quite . . . I was grievously in error, Yakov Petrovitch."

"You say so?" Mr. Golyadkin's perfidious friend inquired, rather casually and indifferently.

"I say that I was quite in error, Yakov Petrovitch, and that for my part, quite without false shame, I am . . ."

"Ah, well, that's all right! That's a nice thing your being in error," answered Mr. Golyadkin junior.

"I even had an idea, Yakov Petrovitch," our candid hero answered in a gentlemanly way, completely failing to observe the horrible perfidy of his deceitful enemy; "I even had an idea that here were two people created exactly alike. . . ."

"Ah, is that your idea?"

At this point the notoriously worthless Mr. Golyadkin took up his hat. Still failing to observe his treachery, Mr. Golyadkin senior, too, got up and with a noble, simple-hearted smile to his false friend, tried in his innocence to be friendly to him, to encourage him, and in that way to form a new friendship with him.

"Goody-bye, your Excellency," Mr. Golyadkin junior called out suddenly. Our hero started, noticing in his enemy's face something positively Bacchanalian, and, solely to get rid of him, put two fingers into the unprincipled man's outstretched hand; but then . . . then his enemy's shamelessness passed all bounds. Seizing the two fingers of Mr. Golyadkin's hand and at first pressing them, the worthless fellow on the spot, before Mr. Golyadkin's eyes, had the effrontery to repeat the shameful joke of the morning. The limit of human patience was exhausted.

He had just hidden in his pocket the handkerchief with which he had wiped his fingers when Mr.Golyadkin senior recovered from the shock and dashed after him into the next room, into which his irreconcilable foe had in his usual hasty way hastened to decamp. As though perfectly innocent, he was standing at the counter eating pies, and with perfect composure, like a virtuous man, was making polite remarks to the German woman behind the counter.

"I can't go into it before ladies," thought our hero, and he, too, went up to the counter, so agitated that he hardly knew what he was doing.

"The tart is certainly not bad! What do you think?" Mr. Golyadkin junior began upon his unseemly sallies again, reckoning, no doubt, upon Mr. Golyadkin's infinite patience. The stout German, for her part, looked at both her visitors with pewtery, vacant-looking eyes, smiling affably and evidently not understanding Russian. Our hero flushed red as fire at the words of the unabashed Mr. Golyadkin junior, and, unable to control himself, rushed at him with the evident intention of tearing him to pieces and finishing off completely, but Mr. Golyadkin junior, in his usual mean way, was already far off; he took flight, he was already on the steps. It need hardly be said that, after the first moment of stupefaction with which Mr. Golyadkin senior was naturally overcome, he recovered himself and went at full speed after his insulting enemy, who had already got into a cab, whose driver was obviously in collusion with him. But at that very instant the stout German, seeing both her customers make off, shrieked and rang her bell with all her might. Our hero was on the point of flight, but he turned back, and, without asking for change, flung her money for himself and for the shameless man who had left without paying, and although thus delayed he succeeded in catching up his enemy. Hanging on to the side of the cab with all the force bestowed on him by nature, our hero was carried for some time along the street, clambering upon the vehicle, while Mr. Golyadkin junior did his utmost to dislodge him. Meanwhile the cabman, with whip, with reins, with kicks and with shouts urged on his exhausted nag, who quite unexpectedly dropped into a gallop, biting at the bit, and kicking with his hind legs in a horrid way. At last our hero succeeded in climbing into the cab, facing his enemy and with his back to the driver, his knees touching the knees and his right hand clutching the very shabby fur collar of his depraved and exasperated foe.

The enemies were borne along for some time in silence. Our hero could scarcely breathe. It was a bad road and he was jolted at every step and in peril of breaking his neck. Moreover, his exasperated foe still refused to acknowledge himself vanquished and was trying to shove him off into the mud. To complete the unpleasantness of his position the weather was detestable. The snow was falling in heavy flakes and doing its utmost to creep under the unfastened overcoat of the genuine Mr. Golyadkin. It was foggy and nothing could be seen. It was difficult to tell through what street and in what direction they were being taken. . . . It seemed to Mr. Golyadkin that what was happening to him was somehow familiar. One instant he tried to remember whether he had had a presentiment of it the day before, in a dream, for instance. . . .

At last his wretchedness reached the utmost pitch of agony. Leaning upon his merciless opponent, he was beginning to cry out. But his cries died away upon his lips. . . . There was a moment when Mr. Golyadkin forgot everything, and made up his mind that all this was of no consequence and that it was all nothing, that it was happening in some inexplicable manner, and that, therefore, to protest was effort thrown away. . . . But suddenly and almost at the same instant that our hero was drawing this conclusion, an unexpected jolt gave quite a new turn to the affair. Mr. Golyadkin fell off the cab like a sack of flour and rolled on the ground, quite correctly recognizing, at the moment of his fall, that his excitement had been very inappropriate. Jumping up at last, he saw that they had arrived somewhere; the cab was standing in the middle of some courtyard, and from the first glance our hero noticed that it was the courtyard of the house in which was Olsufy Ivanovitch's flat. At the same instant he noticed that his enemy was mounting the steps, probably on his way to Olsufy Ivanovitch's. In indescribable misery he was about to pursue his enemy, but, fortunately for himself, prudently thought better of it. Not forgetting to pay the cabman, Mr. Golyadkin

ran with all his might along the street, regardless of where he was going.
The snow was falling heavily as before; as before it was muggy, wet, and
dark. Our hero did not walk, but flew, coming into collision with every
one on the way—men, women and children, and himself rebounding
from every one—men, women and children. About him and after him
he heard frightened voices, squeals, screams. . . . But Mr. Golyadkin
seemed unconscious and would pay no heed to anything. . . . He came
to himself, however, on Semyonovsky Bridge, and then only through
succeeding in tripping against and upsetting two peasant women and
the wares they were selling, and tumbling over them.

"That's no matter," thought Mr. Golyadkin, "that can easily be set
right," and he felt in his pocket at once, intending to make up for the
cakes, apples, nuts and various trifles he had scattered, with a rouble.
Suddenly a new light dawned upon Mr. Golyadkin; in his pocket he felt
the letter given him in the morning by the clerk. Remembering that
there was a tavern he knew close by, he ran to it without a moment's
delay, settled himself at a little table lighted up by a tallow candle, and,
taking no notice of anything, regardless of the waiter who came to ask
for his orders, broke the seal and began reading the following letter,
which completely astounded him—

"You noble man, who are suffering for my sake, and will be dear
to my heart for ever!

"I am suffering, I am perishing—save me! The slanderer, the
intriguer, notorious for the immorality of his tendencies, has entangled
me in his snares and I am undone! I am lost! But he is abhorrent to me,
while you! . . . They have separated us, they have intercepted my letters
to you—and all this has been the work of the vicious man who has
taken advantage of his one good quality—his likeness to you. A man
can always be plain in appearance, yet fascinate by his intelligence, his
strong feelings and his agreeable manners. . . . I am ruined! I am being
married against my will, and the chief part in this intrigue is taken by
my parent, benefactor and civil councillor, Olsufy Ivanovitch, no doubt
desirous of securing me a place and relations in well-bred society. . . .
But I have made up my mind and I protest by all the powers bestowed
on me by nature. Be waiting for me with a carriage at nine o'clock this
evening at the window of Olsufy Ivanovitch's flat. We are having another ball and a handsome lieutenant is coming. I will come out and we
will fly. Moreover, there are other government offices in which one can
be of service to one's country. In any case, remember, my friend, that

innocence is strong in its very innocence. Farewell. Wait with the carriage at the entrance. I shall throw myself into the protection of your
arms at two o'clock in the night.

> "Yours till death,
> "KLARA OLSUFYEVNA."

After reading the letter our hero remained for some minutes as
though petrified. In terrible anxiety, in terrible agitation, white as a
sheet, with the letter in his hand, he walked several times up and down
the room; to complete the unpleasantness of his position, though our
hero failed to observe it, he was at that moment the object of the exclusive attention of every one in the room. Probably the disorder of his
attire, his unrestrained excitement, his walking, or rather running about
the room, his gesticulating with both hands, perhaps some enigmatic
words unconsciously addressed to the air, probably all this prejudiced
Mr. Golyadkin in the opinion of the customers, and even the waiter
began to look at him suspiciously. Coming to himself, Mr. Golyadkin
noticed that he was standing in the middle of the room and was in an
almost unseemly, discourteous manner staring at an old man of very
respectable appearance who, having dined and said grace before the
ikon, had sat down again and fixed his eyes upon Mr. Golyadkin. Our
hero looked vaguely about him and noticed that every one, actually
every one, was looking at him with a hostile and suspicious air. All at
once a retired military man in a red collar asked loudly for the *Police
News*. Mr. Golyadkin started and turned crimson: he happened to look
down and saw that he was in such disorderly attire as he would not have
worn even at home, much less in a public place. His boots, his trousers
and the whole of his left side were covered with mud; the trouser-strap
was torn off his right foot, and his coat was even torn in many places. In
extreme misery our hero went up to the table at which he had read the
letter, and saw that the attendant was coming up to him with a strange
and impudently peremptory expression of face. Utterly disconcerted
and crestfallen, our hero began to look about the table at which he was
now standing. On the table stood a dirty plate, left there from somebody's dinner, a soiled table-napkin and a knife, fork and spoon that had
just been used. "Who has been having dinner?" thought our hero. "Can
it have been I? Anything is possible! I must have had dinner without
noticing it; what am I to do?"

Raising his eyes, Mr. Golyadkin again saw beside him the waiter who
was about to address him.

"How much is my bill, my lad?" our hero inquired, in a trembling voice.

A loud laugh sounded round Mr. Golyadkin, the waiter himself grinned. Mr. Golyadkin realized that he had blundered again, and had done something dreadfully stupid. He was overcome by confusion, and to avoid standing there with nothing to do he put his hand in his pocket to get out his handkerchief; but to the indescribable amazement of himself and all surrounding him, he pulled out instead of his handkerchief the bottle of medicine which Krestyan Ivanovitch had prescribed for him four days earlier. "Get the medicine at the same chemist's," floated through Mr. Golyadkin's brain. . . .

Suddenly he started and almost cried out in horror. A new light dawned. . . . The dark reddish and repulsive liquid had a sinister gleam to Mr. Golyadkin's eyes. . . . The bottle dropped from his hands and was instantly smashed. Our hero cried out and stepped back a pace to avoid the spilled medicine . . . he was trembling in every limb, and drops of sweat came out on to his brow and temples. "So my life is in danger!" Meantime there was a stir, a commotion in the room; every one surrounded Mr. Golyadkin, every one talked to Mr. Golyadkin, some even caught hold of Mr. Golyadkin. But our hero was dumb and motionless, seeing nothing, hearing nothing, feeling nothing. . . . At last, as though tearing himself from the place, he rushed out of the tavern, pushing away all and each who tried to detain him; almost unconscious, he got into the first cab that passed him and drove to his flat.

In the entry of his flat he met Mihyeev, an attendant from the office, with an official envelope in his hand.

"I know, my good man, I know all about it," our exhausted hero answered, in a weak, miserable voice; "it's official . . ."

The envelope did, in fact, contain instructions to Mr. Golyadkin, signed by Andrey Filippovitch, to give up the business in his hands to Ivan Semyonovitch. Taking the envelope and giving ten kopecks to the man, Mr. Golyadkin went into his flat and saw that Petrushka was collecting all his odds and ends, all his things into a heap, evidently intending to abandon Mr. Golyadkin and move to the flat of Karolina Ivanovna, who had enticed him to take the place of Yevstafy.

CHAPTER XII

PETRUSHKA came in swaggering, with a strangely casual manner and an air of vulgar triumph on his face. It was evident that he had some idea in his head, that he felt thoroughly within his rights, and he looked like an unconcerned spectator—that is, as though he were anybody's servant rather than Mr. Golyadkin's.

"I say, you know, my good lad," our hero began breathlessly, "what time is it?"

Without speaking, Petrushka went behind his partition, then returned, and in a rather independent tone announced that it was nearly half-past seven.

"Well, that's all right, my lad, that's all right. Come, you see, my boy . . . allow me to tell you, my good lad, that everything, I fancy, is at an end between us."

Petrushka said nothing.

"Well, now as everything is over between us, tell me openly, as a friend, where you have been."

"Where I've been? To see good people, sir."

"I know, my good lad, I know. I have always been satisfied with you, and I give you a character. . . . Well, what are you doing with them now?"

"Why, sir! You know yourself. We all know a decent man won't teach you any harm."

"I know, my dear fellow, I know. Nowadays good people are rare, my lad; prize them, my friend. Well, how are they?"

"To be sure, they . . . Only I can't serve you any longer, sir; as your honour must know."

"I know, my dear fellow, I know your zeal and devotion; I have seen it all, my lad, I've noticed it. I respect you, my friend. I respect a good and honest man, even though he's a lackey."

"Why, yes, to be sure! The likes of us, of course, as you know yourself, are as good as anybody. That's so. We all know, sir, there's no getting on without a good man."

"Very well, very well, my boy, I feel it. . . . Come, here's your money and here's your character. Now we'll kiss and say good-bye, brother. . . . Come, now, my lad, I'll ask one service of you, one last service," said Mr. Golyadkin, in a solemn voice. "You see, my dear boy, all sorts of things happen. Sorrow is concealed in gilded palaces, and there's no escaping it. You know, my boy, I've always been kind to you, my boy."

Petrushka remained mute.

"I believe I've always been kind to you, my dear fellow. . . . Come, how much linen have we now, my dear boy?"

"Well, it's all there. Linen shirts six, three pairs of socks; four shirt-fronts; flannel vests; of underlinen two sets. You know all that yourself. I've got nothing of yours, sir. . . . I look after my master's belongings, sir. I am like that, sir . . . we all know . . . and I've . . . never been guilty of anything of the sort, sir, you know yourself, sir . . ."

"I trust you, my lad, I trust you. I didn't mean that, my friend, I didn't mean that, you know, my lad; I tell you what . . ."

"To be sure, sir, we know that already. Why, when I used to be in service at General Stolbnyakov's . . . I lost the place through the family's going away to Saratov . . . they've an estate there . . ."

"No; I didn't mean that, my lad, I didn't mean that; don't think anything of the sort, my dear fellow . . ."

"To be sure. It's easy, as you know yourself, sir, to take away the character of folks like us. And I've always given satisfaction—ministers, generals, senators, counts—I've served them all. I've been at Prince Svintchatkin's, at Colonel Pereborkin's, at General Nedobarov's—they've gone away too, they've gone to their property. As we all know . . ."

"Yes, my lad, very good, my lad, very good. And now I'm going away, my friend. . . . A different path lies before each man, no one can tell what road he may have to take. Come, my lad, put out my clothes now, lay out my uniform too . . . and my other trousers, my sheets, quilts and pillows . . ."

"Am I to pack them all in the bag?"

"Yes, my lad, yes; the bag, please. Who knows what may happen to us. Come, my dear boy, you can go and find a carriage . . ."

"A carriage? . . ."

"Yes, my lad, a carriage; a roomy one, and take it by the hour. And don't you imagine anything . . ."

"And are you meaning to go far away, sir?"

"I don't know, my lad, I don't know that either. I think you had better pack my feather bed too. What do you think, my lad? I am relying on you, my dear fellow . . ."

"Is your honour setting off at once?"

"Yes, my friend, yes! Circumstances have turned out so . . . so it is, my dear fellow, so it is . . ."

"To be sure, sir; when we were in the regiment the same thing happened to the lieutenant; they eloped from a country gentleman's . . ."

"Eloped? . . . How! My dear fellow!"

"Yes, sir, eloped, and they were married in another house. Everything was got ready beforehand. There was a hue and cry after them; the late prince took their part, and so it was all settled . . ."

"They were married, but . . . how is it, my dear fellow. . . . How did you come to know, my boy?"

"Why, to be sure! The earth is full of rumours, sir. We know, sir, we've all . . . to be sure, there's no one without sin. Only I'll tell you now, sir, let me speak plainly and vulgarly, sir; since it has come to this, I must tell you, sir; you have an enemy—you've a rival, sir, a powerful rival, so there . . ."

"I know, my dear fellow, I know; you know yourself, my dear fellow. . . . So, you see, I'm relying upon you. What are we to do now, my friend! How do you advise me?"

"Well, sir, if you are in that way now, if you've come, so to say, to such a pass, sir, you'll have to make some purchases, sir—say some sheets, pillows, another feather bed, a double one, a good quilt—here at the neighbours' downstairs—she's a shopkeeper, sir—she has a good fox-fur cloak, so you might look at it and buy it, you might have a look at it at once. You'll need it now, sir; it's a good cloak, sir, satin-lined with fox . . ."

"Very good, my lad, very good, I agree; I rely upon you, I rely upon you entirely; a cloak by all means, if necessary. . . . Only make haste, make haste! For God's sake make haste! I'll buy the cloak—only please make haste! It will soon be eight o'clock. Make haste for God's sake, my dear lad! Hurry up, my lad . . ."

Petrushka ran to gather together a bundle of linen, pillows, quilt, sheets, and all sorts of odds and ends, tied them up and rushed headlong out of the room. Meanwhile, Mr. Golyadkin seized the letter once more, but he could not read it. Clutching his devoted head, he leaned against the wall in a state of stupefaction. He could not think of anything, he could do nothing either, and could not even tell what was happening to him. At last, seeing that time was passing and neither Petrushka nor the fur cloak had made their appearance, Mr. Golyadkin made up his mind to go himself. Opening the door into the entry, he heard below noise, talk, disputing, scuffling. . . . Several of the women of the neighbouring flats were shouting, talking and protesting about something—Mr. Golyadkin knew what. Petrushka's voice was heard: then there was a sound of footsteps.

"My goodness! They'll bring all the world in here," moaned Mr. Golyadkin, wringing his hands in despair and rushing back into his

room. Running back into his room, he fell almost senseless on the sofa
with his face in the pillow. After lying a minute in this way, he jumped
up and, without waiting for Petrushka, he put on his goloshes, his hat
and his greatcoat, snatched up his papers and ran headlong downstairs.

"Nothing is wanted, nothing, my dear fellow! I will manage myself—
everything myself. I don't need you for the time, and meantime, things
may take a better turn, perhaps," Mr. Golyadkin muttered to Petrushka,
meeting him on the stairs; then he ran out into the yard, away from the
house. There was a faintness at his heart, he had not yet made up his
mind what was his position, what he was to do, how he was to act in the
present critical position.

"Yes, how am I to act? Lord, have mercy on me! And that all this
should happen!" he cried out at last in despair, tottering along the street
at random; "that all this must needs happen! Why, but for this, but for
just this, everything would have been put right; at one stroke, at one
skilful, vigorous, firm stroke it would have been set right. I would have
my finger cut off to have it set right! And I know, indeed, how it would
have been settled. This is how it would have been managed: I'd have
gone on the spot . . . said how it was . . . 'with your permission, sir, I'm
neither here nor there in it . . . things aren't done like that,' I would say,
'my dear sir, things aren't done like that, there's no accepting an impostor in our office; an impostor . . . my dear sir, is a man . . . who is worthless and of no service to his country. Do you understand that? Do you
understand that, my dear sir,' I should say! That's how it would be. . . .
But no . . . after all, things are not like that . . . not a bit like that. . . . I
am talking nonsense, like a fool! A suicidal fool! It's not like that at all,
you suicidal fool. . . . This is how things are done, though, you profli-
gate man! . . . Well, what am I to do with myself now? Well, what am I
going to do with myself now. What am I fit for now? Come, what are
you fit for now, for instance, you, Golyadkin, you, you worthless fellow!
Well, what now? I must get a carriage; 'hire a carriage and bring it here,'
says she, 'we shall get our feet wet without a carriage,' says she. . . . And
who could ever have thought it! Fie, fie, my young lady! Fie, fie, a
young lady of virtuous behaviour! Well, well, the girl we all thought so
much of! You've distinguished yourself, madam, there's no doubt of
that! you've distinguished yourself! . . . And it all comes from immoral
education. And now that I've looked into it and seen through it all I see
that it is due to nothing else but immorality. Instead of looking after her
as a child . . . and the rod at times . . . they stuff her with sweets and
dainties, and the old man is always doting over her: saying 'my dear, my
love, my beauty,' saying, 'we'll marry you to a count!' . . . And now she

has come forward herself and shown her cards, as though to say that's her little game! Instead of keeping her at home as a child, they sent her to a boarding-school, to a French madame, an *émigrée*, a Madame Falbalas or something, and she learned all sorts of things at that Madame Falbalas', and this is how it always turns out. 'Come,' says she, 'and be happy! Be in a carriage,' she says, 'at such a time, under the windows, and sing a sentimental serenade in the Spanish style; I await you and I know you love me, and we will fly together and live in a hut.' But the fact is it's impossible; since it has come to that, madam, it's impossible, it is against the law to abduct an innocent, respectable girl from her parents' roof without their sanction! And, if you come to that, why, what for and what need is there to do it? Come, she should marry a suitable person, the man marked out by destiny, and that would be the end of it. But I'm in the government service, I might lose my berth through it: I might be arrested for it, madam! I tell you that! If you did not know it. It's that German woman's doing. She's at the bottom of it all, the witch; she cooked the whole kettle of fish. For they've slandered a man, for they've invented a bit of womanish gossip about him, a regular performance by the advice of Andrey Filippovitch, that's what it came from. Otherwise how could Petrushka be mixed up in it? What has he to do with it? What need for that rogue to be in it? No, I cannot, madam, I cannot possibly, not on any account. . . . No, madam, this time you must really excuse me. It's all your doing, madam, it's not all the German's doing, it's not the witch's doing at all, but simply yours. For the witch is a good woman, for the witch is not to blame in any way; it's your fault, madam; it's you who are to blame, let me tell you! I shall be charged with a crime through you, madam. . . . A man might be ruined . . . a man might lose sight of himself, and not be able to restrain himself—a wedding, indeed! And how is it all going to end? And how will it all be arranged? I would give a great deal to know all that! . . ."

So our hero reflected in his despair. Coming to himself suddenly, he observed that he was standing somewhere in Liteyny Street. The weather was awful: it was a thaw; snow and rain were falling—just as at that memorable time when at the dread hour of midnight all Mr. Golyadkin's troubles had begun. "This is a nice night for a journey!" thought Mr. Golyadkin, looking at the weather; "it's death all round. . . . Good Lord! Where am I to find a carriage, for instance? I believe there's something black there at the corner. We'll see, we'll investigate. . . . Lord, have mercy on us!" our hero went on, bending his weak and tottering steps in the direction in which he saw something that looked like a cab.

"No, I know what I'll do; I'll go straight and fall on my knees, if I can, and humbly beg, saying 'I put my fate in your hands, in the hands of my superiors'; saying, 'Your Excellency, be a protector and a benefactor'; and then I'll say this and that, and explain how it is and that it is an unlawful act; 'Do not destroy me, I look upon you as my father, do not abandon me . . . save my dignity, my honour, my name, my reputation . . . and save me from a miscreant, a vicious man. . . . He's another person, your Excellency, and I'm another person too; he's apart and I am myself by myself too; I am really myself by myself, your Excellency; really myself by myself,' that's what I shall say. 'I cannot be like him. Change him, dismiss him, give orders for him to be changed and a godless, licentious impersonation to be suppressed . . . that it may not be an example to others, your Excellency. I look upon you as a father'; those in authority over us, our benefactors and protectors, are bound, of course, to encourage such impulses. . . . There's something chivalrous about it: I shall say, 'I look upon you, my benefactor and superior, as a father, and trust my fate to you, and I will not say anything against it; I put myself in your hands, and retire from the affair myself' . . . that's what I would say."

"Well, my man, are you a cabman?"

"Yes . . ."

"I want a cab for the evening . . ."

"And does your honour want to go far?"

"For the evening, for the evening; wherever I have to go, my man, wherever I have to go."

"Does your honour want to drive out of town?"

"Yes, my friend, out of town, perhaps. I don't quite know myself yet, I can't tell you for certain, my man. Maybe you see it will all be settled for the best. We all know, my friend . . ."

"Yes, sir, of course we all know. Please God it may."

"Yes, my friend, yes; thank you, my dear fellow; come, what's your fare, my good man? . . ."

"Do you want to set off at once?"

"Yes, at once, that is, no, you must wait at a certain place. . . . A little while, not long, you'll have to wait . . ."

"Well, if you hire me for the whole time, I couldn't ask less than six roubles for weather like this . . ."

"Oh, very well, my friend; and I thank you, my dear fellow. So, come, you can take me now, my good man."

"Get in; allow me, I'll put it straight a bit—now will your honour get in. Where shall I drive?"

"To the Ismailovsky Bridge, my friend."

The driver plumped down on the box, with difficulty roused his pair of lean nags from the trough of hay, and was setting off for Ismailovsky Bridge. But suddenly Mr. Golyadkin pulled the cord, stopped the cab, and besought him in an imploring voice not to drive to Ismailovsky Bridge, but to turn back to another street. The driver turned into another street, and ten minutes later Mr. Golyadkin's newly hired equipage was standing before the house in which his Excellency had a flat. Mr. Golyadkin got out of the carriage, begged the driver to be sure to wait and with a sinking heart ran upstairs to the third storey and pulled the bell; the door was opened and our hero found himself in the entry of his Excellency's flat.

"Is his Excellency graciously pleased to be at home?" said Mr. Golyadkin, addressing the man who opened the door.

"What do you want?" asked the servant, scrutinizing Mr. Golyadkin from head to foot.

"I, my friend . . . I am Golyadkin, the titular councillor, Golyadkin. . . . To say . . . something or other . . . to explain . . ."

"You must wait; you cannot . . ."

"My friend, I cannot wait; my business is important, it's business that admits of no delay . . ."

"But from whom have you come? Have you brought papers? . . ."

"No, my friend, I am on my own account. Announce me, my friend, say something or other, explain. I'll reward you, my good man . . ."

"I cannot. His Excellency is not at home, he has visitors. Come at ten o'clock in the morning . . ."

"Take in my name, my good man, I can't wait—it is impossible. . . . You'll have to answer for it, my good man."

"Why, go and announce him! What's the matter with you; want to save your shoe leather?" said another lackey, who was lolling on the bench and had not uttered a word till then.

"Shoe leather! I was told not to show any one up, you know; their time is the morning."

"Announce him, have you lost your tongue?"

"I'll announce him all right—I've not lost my tongue. It's not my orders; I've told you, it's not my orders. Walk inside."

Mr. Golyadkin went into the outermost room; there was a clock on the table. He glanced at it: it was half-past eight. His heart ached within him. Already he wanted to turn back, but at that very moment the footman standing at the door of the next room had already boomed out Mr. Golyadkin's name.

"Oh, what lungs," thought our hero in indescribable misery. "Why, you ought to have said: 'he has come most humbly and meekly to make an explanation . . . something . . . be graciously pleased to see him.' . . . Now the whole business is ruined; all my hopes are scattered to the winds. But . . . however . . . never mind. . . ."

There was no time to think, moreover. The lackey, returning, said, "Please walk in," and led Mr. Golyadkin into the study.

When our hero went in, he felt as though he were blinded, for he could see nothing at all. . . . But three or four figures seemed flitting before his eyes: "Oh, yes, they are the visitors," flashed through Mr. Golyadkin's mind. At last our hero could distinguish clearly the star on the black coat of his Excellency, then by degrees advanced to seeing the black coat and at last gained the power of complete vision. . . .

"What is it?" said a familiar voice above Mr. Golyadkin.

"The titular councillor, Golyadkin, your Excellency."

"Well?"

"I have come to make an explanation . . ."

"How? . . . What?"

"Why, yes. This is how it is. I've come for an explanation, your Excellency . . ."

"But you . . . but who are you? . . ."

"M—m—m—mist—er Golyadkin, your Excellency, a titular councillor."

"Well, what is it you want?"

"Why, this is how it is, I look upon you as a father; I retire . . . defend me from my enemy! . . ."

"What's this? . . ."

"We all know . . ."

"What do we all know?"

Mr. Golyadkin was silent: his chin began twitching a little.

"Well?"

"I thought it was chivalrous, your Excellency. . . . 'There's something chivalrous in it,' I said, 'and I look upon my superior as a father' . . . this is what I thought; 'protect me, I tear . . . earfully . . . b . . . beg and that such imp . . . impulses ought . . . to . . . be encouraged . . .'"

His Excellency turned away, our hero for some minutes could distinguish nothing. There was a weight on his chest. His breathing was laboured; he did not know where he was standing. . . . He felt ashamed and sad. God knows what followed. . . . Recovering himself, our hero noticed that his Excellency was talking with his guests, and seemed to be briskly and emphatically discussing something with them. One of the visitors Mr. Golyadkin recognized at once. This was Andrey Filippovitch;

he knew no one else; yet there was another person that seemed familiar—a tall, thick-set figure, middle-aged, possessed of very thick eyebrows and whiskers and a significant sharp expression. On his chest was an order and in his mouth a cigar. This gentleman was smoking and nodding significantly without taking the cigar out of his mouth, glancing from time to time at Mr. Golyadkin. Mr. Golyadkin felt awkward; he turned away his eyes and immediately saw another very strange visitor. Through a door which our hero had taken for a looking-glass, just as he had done once before—*he* made his appearance—we know who: a very intimate friend and acquaintance of Mr. Golyadkin's. Mr. Golyadkin junior had actually been till then in a little room close by, hurriedly writing something; now, apparently, he was needed—and he came in with papers under his arm, went up to his Excellency, and while waiting for exclusive attention to be paid him succeeded very adroitly in putting his spoke into the talk and consultation, taking his place a little behind Andrey Filippovitch's back and partly screening him from the gentleman smoking the cigar. Apparently Mr. Golyadkin junior took an extreme interest in the conversation, to which he was listening now in a gentlemanly way, nodding his head, fidgeting with his feet, smiling, continually looking at his Excellency—as it were beseeching him with his eyes to let him put his word in.

"The scoundrel," thought Mr. Golyadkin, and involuntarily he took a step forward. At this moment his Excellency turned round, and came rather hesitatingly towards Mr. Golyadkin.

"Well, that's all right, that's all right; well, run along, now. I'll look into your case, and give orders for you to be taken . . ."

At this point his Excellency glanced at the gentleman with the thick whiskers. The latter nodded in assent.

Mr. Golyadkin felt and distinctly understood that they were taking him for something different and not looking at him in the proper light at all.

"In one way or another I must explain myself," he thought; "I must say, 'This is how it is, your Excellency.'"

At this point in his perplexity he dropped his eyes to the floor and to his great astonishment he saw a good-sized patch of something white on his Excellency's boots.

"Can there be a hole in them?" thought Mr. Golyadkin. Mr. Golyadkin was, however, soon convinced that his Excellency's boots were not split, but were only shining brilliantly—a phenomenon fully explained by the fact that they were patent leather and highly polished.

"It is what they call *blick*," thought our hero; "the term is used par-

ticularly in artists' studios; in other places such a reflected light is called
a rib of light."

At this point Mr. Golyadkin raised his eyes and saw that the time had
come to speak, for things might easily end badly. . . .

Our hero took a step forward.

"I say this is how it is, your Excellency," he said, "and there's no
accepting impostors nowadays."

His Excellency made no answer, but rang the bell violently. Our
hero took another step forward.

"He is a vile, vicious man, your Excellency," said our hero, beside
himself and faint with terror, though he still pointed boldly and resolutely at his unworthy twin, who was fidgeting about near his Excellency. "I say this is how it is, and I am alluding to a well-known person."

There was a general sensation at Mr. Golyadkin's words. Andrey Filippovitch and the gentleman with the cigar nodded their heads; his
Excellency impatiently tugged at the bell to summon the servants. At
this point Mr. Golyadkin junior came forward in his turn.

"Your Excellency," he said, "I humbly beg permission to speak."
There was something very resolute in Mr. Golyadkin junior's voice;
everything showed that he felt himself completely in the right.

"Allow me to ask you," he began again, anticipating his Excellency's
reply in his eagerness, and this time addressing Mr. Golyadkin; "allow
me to ask you, in whose presence you are making this explanation?
Before whom are you standing, in whose room are you? . . ."

Mr. Golyadkin junior was in a state of extraordinary excitement,
flushed and glowing with wrath and indignation; there were positively
tears in his eyes.

A lackey, appearing in the doorway, roared at the top of his voice the
name of some new arrivals, the Bassavryukovs.

"A good aristocratic name, hailing from Little Russia," thought Mr.
Golyadkin, and at that moment he felt some one lay a very friendly
hand on his back, then a second hand was laid on his back. Mr. Golyadkin's infamous twin was tripping about in front leading the way; and our
hero saw clearly that he was being led to the big doors of the room.

"Just as it was at Olsufy Ivanovitch's," he thought, and he found himself in the hall. Looking round, he saw beside him two of his Excellency's lackeys and his twin.

"The greatcoat, the greatcoat, the greatcoat, the greatcoat, my friend!
The greatcoat of my best friend!" whispered the depraved man, snatch-
ing the coat from one of the servants, and by way of a nasty and
ungentlemanly joke flinging it straight at Mr. Golyadkin's head. Extri-

cating himself from under his coat, Mr. Golyadkin distinctly heard the two lackeys snigger. But without listening to anything, or paying attention to it, he went out of the hall and found himself on the lighted stairs, Mr. Golyadkin junior following him.

"Good-bye, your Excellency!" he shouted after Mr. Golyadkin senior.

"Scoundrel!" our hero exclaimed, beside himself.

"Well, scoundrel, then . . ."

"Depraved man! . . ."

"Well, depraved man, then . . ." answered Mr. Golyadkin's unworthy enemy, and with his characteristic baseness he looked down from the top of the stairs straight into Mr. Golyadkin's face as though begging him to go on. Our hero spat with indignation and ran out of the front door; he was so shattered, so crushed, that he had no recollection of how he got into the cab or who helped him in. Coming to himself, he found that he was being driven to Fontanka. "To Ismailovsky Bridge, then," thought Mr. Golyadkin. At this point Mr. Golyadkin tried to think of something else, but could not; there was something so terrible that he could not explain it. . . . "Well, never mind," our hero concluded, and he drove to Ismailovsky Bridge.

CHAPTER XIII

. . . IT seemed as though the weather meant to change for the better. The snow, which had till then been coming down in regular clouds, began growing less and less and at last almost ceased. The sky became visible and here and there tiny stars sparkled in it. It was only wet, muddy, damp and stifling, especially for Mr. Golyadkin, who could hardly breathe as it was. His greatcoat, soaked and heavy with wet, sent a sort of unpleasant warm dampness all through him and weighed down his exhausted legs. A feverish shiver sent sharp, shooting pains all over him; he was in a painful cold sweat of exhaustion, so much so that Mr. Golyadkin even forgot to repeat at every suitable occasion with his characteristic firmness and resolution his favourite phrase that "it all, maybe, most likely, indeed, might turn out for the best." "But all this does not matter for the time," our hero repeated, still staunch and not downhearted, wiping from his face the cold drops that streamed in all directions from the brim of his round hat, which was so soaked that it could hold no more water. Adding that all this was nothing so far, our hero tried to sit on a rather thick clump of wood, which was lying near a heap of logs in Olsufy Ivanovitch's yard. Of course, it was no good thinking of Spanish serenades or silken ladders, but it was quite necessary to think of a modest corner, snug and private, if not altogether warm. He felt greatly tempted, we may mention in passing, by that corner in the back entry of Olsufy Ivanovitch's flat in which he had once, almost at the beginning of this true story, stood for two hours between a cupboard and an old screen among all sorts of domestic odds and ends and useless litter. The fact is that Mr. Golyadkin had been standing waiting for two whole hours on this occasion in Olsufy Ivanovitch's yard. But in regard to that modest and snug little corner there were certain drawbacks which had not existed before. The first drawback was the fact that it was probably now a marked place and that certain precautionary measures had been taken in regard to it since the scandal at Olsufy Ivanovitch's last ball. Secondly, he had to wait for a signal from Klara Olsufyevna, for there was bound to be some such signal, it was always a feature in such cases and, "it didn't begin with us and it won't end with us."

At this point Mr. Golyadkin very appropriately remembered a novel he had read long ago in which the heroine, in precisely similar circumstances, signalled to Alfred by tying a pink ribbon to her window. But now, at night, in the climate of Petersburg, famous for its dampness and unreliability, a pink ribbon was hardly appropriate and, in fact, was utterly out of the question.

"No, it's not a matter of silk ladders," thought our hero, "and I had better stay here quietly and comfortably. . . . I had better stand here."

And he selected a place in the yard exactly opposite the window, near a stack of firewood. Of course, many persons, grooms and coachmen, were continually crossing the yard, and there was, besides, the rumbling of wheels and the snorting of horses and so on; yet it was a convenient place, whether he was observed or not; but now, anyway, there was the advantage of being to some extent in shadow, and no one could see Mr. Golyadkin while he himself could see everything.

The windows were brightly lit up, there was some sort of ceremonious party at Olsufy Ivanovitch's. But he could hear no music as yet.

"So it's not a ball, but a party of some other sort," thought our hero, somewhat aghast. "Is it to-day?" floated the doubt through him. "Have I made a mistake in the date? Perhaps; anything is possible. . . . Yes, to be sure, anything is possible. . . . Perhaps she wrote a letter to me yesterday, and it didn't reach me, and perhaps it did not reach me because Petrushka put his spoke in, the rascal! Or it was to-morrow in the letter, that is, that I . . . should do everything to-morrow, that is—wait with a carriage. . . ."

At this point our hero turned cold all over and felt in his pocket for the letter, to make sure. But to his surprise the letter was not in his pocket.

"How's this?" muttered Mr. Golyadkin, more dead than alive. "Where did I leave it? Then I must have lost it. That is the last straw!" he moaned at last. "Oh, if it falls into evil hands! Perhaps it has already. Good Lord! What may it not lead to! It may lead to something such that . . . Ach, my miserable fate!" At this point Mr. Golyadkin began trembling like a leaf at the thought that perhaps his vicious twin had thrown the greatcoat at him with the object of stealing the letter of which he had somehow got an inkling from Mr. Golyadkin's enemies.

"What's more, he's stealing it," thought our hero, "as evidence . . . but why evidence! . . ."

After the first shock of horror, the blood rushed to Mr. Golyadkin's head. Moaning and gnashing his teeth, he clutched his burning head, sank back on his block of wood and relapsed into brooding. . . . But he could form no coherent thoughts. Figures kept flitting through his brain, incidents came back to his memory, now vaguely, now distinctly, the tunes of some foolish songs kept ringing in his ears. . . . He was in great distress, unnatural distress!

"My God, my God!" our hero thought, recovering himself a little, and suppressing a muffled sob, "give me fortitude in the immensity of my afflictions! That I am done for, utterly destroyed—of that there can be no doubt, and that's all in the natural order of things, since it cannot be otherwise. To begin with, I've lost my berth, I've certainly lost it, I must have lost it. . . . Well, supposing things are set right somehow. Supposing I have money enough to begin with: I must have another lodging, furniture of some sort. . . . In the first place, I shan't have Petrushka. I can get on without the rascal . . . somehow, with help from the people of the house; well, that will be all right! I can go in and out when I like, and Petrushka won't grumble at my coming in late—yes, that is so; that's why it's a good thing to have the people in the house. . . . Well, supposing that's all right; but all that's nothing to do with it, all that's nothing to do with it."

At this point the thought of the real position again dawned upon Mr. Golyadkin's memory. He looked round.

"Oh, Lord, have mercy on me, have mercy on me! What am I talking about?" he thought, growing utterly desperate and clutching his burning head in his hands. . . .

"Won't you soon be going, sir?" a voice pronounced above Mr.

Golyadkin. Our hero started; before him stood his cabman, who was also drenched through and shivering; growing impatient, and having nothing to do, he had thought fit to take a look at Mr. Golyadkin behind the woodstack.

"I am all right, my friend. . . . I am coming soon, soon, very soon; you wait. . . ."

The cabman walked away, grumbling to himself. "What is he grumbling about?" Mr. Golyadkin wondered through his tears. "Why, I have hired him for the evening, why, I'm . . . within my rights now . . . that's so! I've hired him for the evening, and that's the end of it. If one stands still, it's just the same. That's for me to decide. I am free to drive on or not to drive on. And my staying here by the woodstack has nothing to do with the case . . . and don't dare to say anything; think, the gentleman wants to stand behind the woodstack, and so he's standing behind it . . . and he is not disgracing any one's honour! That's the fact of the matter.

"I tell you what it is, madam, if you care to know. Nowadays, madam, nobody lives in a hut, or anything of that sort. No, indeed. And in our industrial age there's no getting on without morality, a fact of which you are a fatal example, madam. . . . You say we must get a job as a register clerk and live in a hut on the sea-shore. In the first place, madam, there are no register clerks on the sea-shore, and in the second place we can't get a job as a register clerk. For supposing, for example, I send in a petition, present myself—saying a register clerk's place or something of the sort . . . and defend me from my enemy . . . they'll tell you, madam, they'll say, to be sure . . . we've lots of register clerks, and here you are not at Madame Falbalas', where you learnt the rules of good behaviour of which you are such a fatal example. Good behaviour, madam, means staying at home, honouring your father and not thinking about suitors prematurely. Suitors will come in good time, madam, that's so! Of course, you are bound to have some accomplishments, such as playing the piano sometimes, speaking French, history, geography, scripture and arithmetic, that's the truth of it! And that's all you need. Cooking, too, cooking certainly forms part of the education of a well-behaved girl! But as it is, in the first place, my fine lady, they won't let you go, they'll raise a hue and cry after you, and then they'll lock you up in a nunnery. How will it be then, madam? What will you have me do then? Would you have me, madam, follow the example of some stupid novels, and melt into tears on a neighbouring hillock, gazing at the cold walls of your prison house, and finally die, following the example of some wretched German poets and novelists. Is that it, madam? But, to begin with, allow me to tell you, as a friend, that things are not done like that, and in the second place I would have given you and your parents, too, a good thrashing for letting you read French books; for French books teach you no good. There's a poison in them . . . a pernicious poison, madam! Or do you imagine, allow me to ask you, or do you imagine that we shall elope with impunity, or something of that sort . . . that we shall have a hut on the shore of the sea and so on; and that we shall begin billing and cooing and talking about our feelings, and that so we shall spend our lives in happiness and content; and then there would be little ones—so then we shall . . . shall go to our father, the civil councillor, Olsufy Ivanovitch, and say 'we've got a little one, and so, on this propitious occasion remove your curse, and bless the couple.' No, madam, I tell you again, that's not the way to do things, and for the first thing there'll be no billing and cooing and please don't reckon on it. Nowadays, madam, the husband is the master and a good, well-brought-up wife should try and please him in every way. And endearments, madam, are not in favour, nowadays, in our industrial age; the day of Jean Jacques Rousseau is over. The husband comes home, for instance, hungry from the office, and asks, 'Isn't there something to eat, my love, a drop of vodka to drink, a bit of salt fish to eat?' So then, madam, you must have the vodka and the herring ready. Your husband will eat it with relish, and he won't so much as look at you, he'll only say 'Run into the kitchen, kitten,' he'll say, 'and look after the dinner,' and at most, once a week, he'll kiss you, even then rather indifferently. . . . That's how it will be with us, my young lady! Yes, even then indifferently. . . . That's how it will be, if one considers it, if it has come to one's looking at the thing in that way. . . . And how do I come in? Why have you mixed me up in your caprices? 'The noble man who is suffering for your sake and will be dear to your heart for ever,' and so on. But in the first place, madam, I am not suited to you, you know yourself, I'm not a great hand at compliments, I'm not fond of uttering perfumed trifles for the ladies. I'm not fond of lady-killers, and I must own I've never been a beauty to look at. You won't find any swagger or false shame in me, and I tell you so now in all sincerity. This is the fact of the matter: we can boast of nothing but a straightforward, open character and common sense; we have nothing to do with intrigues. I am not one to intrigue, I say so and I'm proud of it—that's the fact of the matter! . . . I wear no mask among straightforward people, and to tell you the whole truth . . ."

Suddenly Mr. Golyadkin started. The red and perfectly sopping beard of the cabman appeared round the woodstack again. . . .

"I am coming directly, my friend. I'm coming at once, you know," Mr. Golyadkin responded in a trembling and failing voice.

The cabman scratched his head, then stroked his beard, and moved a step forward . . . stood still and looked suspiciously at Mr. Golyadkin.

"I am coming directly, my friend; you see, my friend . . . I . . . just a little, you see, only a second! . . . more . . . here, you see, my friend. . . ."

"Aren't you coming at all?" the cabman asked at last, definitely coming up to Mr. Golyadkin.

"No, my friend, I'm coming directly. I am waiting, you see, my friend. . . ."

"So I see. . . ."

"You see, my friend, I . . . What part of the country do you come from, my friend?"

"We are under a master . . ."

"And have you a good master? . . ."

"All right. . . ."

"Yes, my friend; you stay here, my friend, you see . . . Have you been in Petersburg long, my friend?"

"It's a year since I came. . . ."

"And are you getting on all right, my friend?"

"Middling."

"To be sure, my friend, to be sure. You must thank Providence, my friend. You must look out for straightforward people. Straightforward people are none too common nowadays, my friend; he would give you washing, food, and drink, my good fellow, a good man would. But sometimes you see tears shed for the sake of gold, my friend . . . you see a lamentable example; that's the fact of the matter, my friend. . . ."

The cabman seemed to feel sorry for Mr. Golyadkin. "Well, your honour, I'll wait. Will your honour be waiting long?"

"No, my friend, no; I . . . you know . . . I won't wait any longer, my good man. . . . What do you think, my friend? I rely upon you. I won't stay any longer."

"Aren't you going at all?"

"No, my friend, no; I'll reward you, my friend . . . that's the fact of the matter. How much ought I to give you, my dear fellow?"

"What you hired me for, please, sir. I've been waiting here a long time; don't be hard on a man, sir."

"Well, here, my good man, here."

At this point Mr. Golyadkin gave six whole roubles to the cabman, and made up his mind in earnest to waste no more time, that is, to clear off straight away, especially as the cabman was dismissed and everything was over, and so it was useless to wait longer. He rushed out of the yard, went out of the gate, turned to the left and without looking round took to his heels, breathless and rejoicing. "Perhaps it will all be for the best," he thought, "and perhaps in this way I've run away from trouble." Mr. Golyadkin suddenly became all at once lighthearted. "Oh, if only it could turn out for the best!" thought our hero, though he put little faith in his own words. "I know what I'll do . . ." he thought. "No, I know, I'd better try the other tack. . . . Or wouldn't it be better to do this? . . ." In this way, hesitating and seeking for the solution of his doubts, our hero ran to Semyonovsky Bridge; but while running to Semyonovsky Bridge he very rationally and conclusively decided to return.

"It will be better so," he thought. "I had better try the other tack, that is . . . I will just go—I'll look on simply as an outsider, and that will be the end of it; I am simply an onlooker, an outsider—and nothing more, whatever happens—it's not my fault, that's the fact of the matter! That's how it shall be now."

Deciding to return, our hero actually did return, the more readily because with this happy thought he conceived of himself now as quite an outsider.

"It's the best thing; one's not responsible for anything, and one will see all that's necessary . . . that's the fact of the matter!"

It was a safe plan and that settled it. Reassured, he crept back under the peaceful shelter of his soothing and protecting woodstack, and began gazing intently at the window. This time he was not destined to gaze and wait for long. Suddenly a strange commotion became apparent at all the windows. Figures appeared, curtains were drawn back, whole groups of people were crowding to the windows at Olsufy Ivanovitch's flat. All were peeping out looking for something in the yard. From the security of his woodstack, our hero, too, began with curiosity watching the general commotion, and with interest craned forward to right and to left so far as he could within the shadow of the woodstack. Suddenly he started, held his breath and almost sat down with horror. It seemed to him—in short, he realized, that they were looking for nothing and for nobody but him, Mr. Golyadkin! Every one was looking in his direction. It was impossible to escape; they saw him. . . . In a flutter, Mr. Golyadkin huddled as closely as he could to the woodstack, and only then noticed that the treacherous shadow had betrayed him, that it did not cover him completely. Our hero would have been delighted at that moment to creep into a mouse-hole in the woodstack, and there meekly to remain, if only it had been possible.

But it was absolutely impossible. In his agony he began at last staring
openly and boldly at the windows, it was the best thing to do. . . . And
suddenly he glowed with shame. He had been fully discovered, every
one was staring at him at once, they were all waving their hands, all
were nodding their heads at him, all were calling to him; then several
windows creaked as they opened, several voices shouted something to
him at once. . . .

"I wonder why they don't whip these naughty girls as children," our
hero muttered to himself, losing his head completely. Suddenly there
ran down the steps *he* (we know who), without his hat or greatcoat,
breathless, rubbing his hands, wriggling, capering, perfidiously displaying intense joy at seeing Mr. Golyadkin.

"Yakov Petrovitch," whispered this individual, so notorious for his
worthlessness, "Yakov Petrovitch, are you here? You'll catch cold. It's
chilly here, Yakov Petrovitch. Come indoors."

"Yakov Petrovitch! No, I'm all right, Yakov Petrovitch," our hero muttered in a submissive voice.

"No, this won't do, Yakov Petrovitch, I beg you, I humbly beg you to
wait with us. 'Make him welcome and bring him in,' they say, 'Yakov
Petrovitch.'"

"No, Yakov Petrovitch, you see, I'd better. . . . I had better go home,
Yakov Petrovitch . . ." said our hero, burning at a slow fire and freezing
at the same time with shame and terror.

"No—no—no—no!" whispered the loathsome person. "No—no—
no, on no account! Come along," he said resolutely, and he dragged
Mr. Golyadkin senior to the steps. Mr. Golyadkin senior did not at all
want to go, but as every one was looking at them, it would have been
stupid to struggle and resist; so our hero went—though, indeed, one
cannot say that he went, because he did not know in the least what was
being done with him. Though, after all, it made no difference!

Before our hero had time to recover himself and come to his senses,
he found himself in the drawing-room. He was pale, dishevelled,
harassed; with lustreless eyes he scanned the crowd—horror! The drawing-room, all the rooms—were full to overflowing. There were masses
of people, a whole galaxy of ladies; and all were crowding round Mr.
Golyadkin, all were pressing towards Mr. Golyadkin, all were squeezing
Mr. Golyadkin and he perceived clearly that they were all forcing him
in one direction.

"Not towards the door," was the thought that floated through Mr.
Golyadkin's mind.

They were, in fact, forcing him not towards the door but Olsufy

Ivanovitch's easy chair. On one side of the armchair stood Klara Olsufyevna, pale, languid, melancholy, but gorgeously dressed. Mr. Golyadkin was particularly struck by a little white flower which rested on her
superb hair. On the other side of the armchair stood Vladimir Semyo-
onovitch, clad in black, with his new order in his buttonhole. Mr.
Golyadkin was led in, as we have described above, straight up to Olsufy Ivanovitch—on one side of him Mr. Golyadkin junior, who had
assumed an air of great decorum and propriety, to the immense relief
of our hero, while on the other side was Andrey Filippovitch, with a
very solemn expression on his face.

"What can it mean?" Mr.Golyadkin wondered.

When he saw that he was being led to Olsufy Ivanovitch, an idea
struck him like a flash of lightning. The thought of the intercepted letter darted through his brain. In great agony our hero stood before Olsufy Ivanovitch's chair.

"What will he say now?" he wondered to himself. "Of course, it will
be all aboveboard now, that is, straightforward and, one may say, honourable; I shall say this is how it is, and so on."

But what our hero apparently feared did not happen. Olsufy
Ivanovitch received Mr. Golyadkin very warmly, and though he did not
hold out his hand to him, yet as he gazed at our hero, he shook his grey
and venerable head—shook it with an air of solemn melancholy and
yet of goodwill. So, at least, it seemed to Mr. Golyadkin. He even fancied that a tear glittered in Olsufy Ivanovitch's lustreless eyes; he raised
his eyes and saw that there seemed to be tears, too, on the eyelashes of
Klara Olsufyevna, who was standing by—that there seemed to be something of the same sort even in the eyes of Vladimir Semyonovitch—that
the unruffled and composed dignity of Andrey Filippovitch had the
same significance as the general tearful sympathy—that even the young
man who was so much like a civil councillor, seizing the opportunity,
was sobbing bitterly. . . . Though perhaps this was only all Mr. Golyadkin's fancy, because he was so much moved himself, and distinctly felt
the hot tears running down his cold cheeks. . . .

Feeling reconciled with mankind and his destiny, and filled with love
at the moment, not only for Olsufy Ivanovitch, not only for the whole
party collected there, but even for his noxious twin (who seemed now
to be by no means noxious, and not even to be his twin at all, but a person very agreeable in himself and in no way connected with him), our
hero, in a voice broken with sobs, tried to express his feelings to Olsufy
Ivanovitch, but was too much overcome by all that he had gone

through, and could not utter a word; he could only, with an expressive gesture, point meekly to his heart . . .

At last, probably to spare the feelings of the old man, Andrey Filippovitch led Mr. Golyadkin a little away, though he seemed to leave him free to do as he liked. Smiling, muttering something to himself, somewhat bewildered, yet almost completely reconciled with fate and his fellow creatures, our hero began to make his way through the crowd of guests. Every one made way for him, every one looked at him with strange curiosity and with mysterious, unaccountable sympathy. Our hero went into another room; he met with the same attention everywhere; he was vaguely conscious of the whole crowd closely following him, noting every step he took, talking in undertones among themselves of something very interesting, shaking their heads, arguing and discussing in whispers. Mr. Golyadkin wanted very much to know what they were discussing in whispers. Looking round, he saw near him Mr. Golyadkin junior. Feeling an overwhelming impulse to seize his hand and draw him aside, Mr. Golyadkin begged the other Yakov Petrovitch most particularly to co-operate with him in all his future undertakings, and not to abandon him at a critical moment. Mr. Golyadkin junior nodded his head gravely and warmly pressed the hand of Mr. Golyadkin senior. Our hero's heart was quivering with the intensity of his emotion. He was gasping for breath, however; he felt so oppressed—so oppressed; he felt that all those eyes fastened upon him were oppressing and dominating him. . . . Mr. Golyadkin caught a glimpse of the councillor who wore a wig. The latter was looking at him with a stern, searching eye, not in the least softened by the general sympathy. . . .

Our hero made up his mind to go straight up to him in order to smile at him and have an immediate explanation, but this somehow did not come off. For one instant Mr. Golyadkin became almost unconscious, almost lost all memory, all feeling.

When he came to himself again he noticed that he was the centre of a large ring formed by the rest of the party round him. Suddenly Mr. Golyadkin's name was called from the other room; the shout was at once taken up by the whole crowd. All was noise and excitement, all rushed to the door of the first room, almost carrying our hero along with them. In the crush the hard-hearted councillor in the wig was side by side with Mr. Golyadkin, and, taking our hero by the hand, he made him sit down beside him opposite Olsufy Ivanovitch, at some distance from the latter, however. Every one in the room sat down; the guests were arranged in rows round Mr. Golyadkin and Olsufy Ivanovitch.

Everything was hushed; every one preserved a solemn silence; every one was watching Olsufy Ivanovitch, evidently expecting something out of the ordinary. Mr. Golyadkin noticed that beside Olsufy Ivanovitch's chair and directly facing the councillor sat Mr. Golyadkin junior, with Andrey Filippovitch. The silence was prolonged; they were evidently expecting something.

"Just as it is in a family when some one is setting off on a far journey. We've only to stand up and pray now," thought our hero.

Suddenly there was a general stir which interrupted Mr. Golyadkin's reflections. Something they had long been waiting for happened.

"He is coming, he is coming!" passed from one to another in the crowd.

"Who is it that is coming?" floated through Mr. Golyadkin's mind, and he shuddered at a strange sensation. "High time too!" said the councillor, looking intently at Andrey Filippovitch. Andrey Filippovitch, for his part, glanced at Olsufy Ivanovitch. Olsufy Ivanovitch gravely and solemnly nodded his head.

"Let us stand up," said the councillor, and he made Mr. Golyadkin get up. All rose to their feet. Then the councillor took Mr. Golyadkin senior by the hand, and Andrey Filippovitch took Mr. Golyadkin junior, and in this way these two precisely similar persons were conducted through the expectant crowd surrounding them. Our hero looked about him in perplexity; but he was at once checked and his attention was called to Mr. Golyadkin junior, who was holding out his hand to him.

"They want to reconcile us," thought our hero, and with emotion he held out his hand to Mr. Golyadkin junior; and then—then bent his head forward towards him. The other Mr. Golyadkin did the same. . . .

At this point it seemed to Mr. Golyadkin senior that his perfidious friend was smiling, that he gave a sly, hurried wink to the crowd of onlookers, and that there was something sinister in the face of the worthless Mr. Golyadkin junior, that he even made a grimace at the moment of his Judas kiss. . . .

There was a ringing in Mr. Golyadkin's ears, and a darkness before his eyes; it seemed to him that an infinite multitude, an unending series of precisely similar Golyadkins were noisily bursting in at every door of the room; but it was too late . . . the resounding, treacherous kiss was over, and . . .

Then quite an unexpected event occurred. . . . The door opened noisily, and in the doorway stood a man, the very sight of whom sent a chill to Mr. Golyadkin's heart. He stood rooted to the spot. A cry of horror died away in his choking throat. Yet Mr. Golyadkin knew it all beforehand, and had had a presentiment of something of the sort for a long time. The new arrival went up to Mr. Golyadkin gravely and solemnly. Mr. Golyadkin knew this personage very well. He had seen him before, had seen him very often, had seen him that day. . . . This personage was a tall, thick-set man in a black dress-coat with a good-sized cross on his breast, and was possessed of thick, very black whiskers; nothing was lacking but the cigar in the mouth to complete the picture. Yet this person's eyes, as we have mentioned already, sent a chill to the heart of Mr. Golyadkin. With a grave and solemn air this terrible man approached the pitiable hero of our story. . . . Our hero held out his hand to him; the stranger took his hand and drew him along with him. . . . With a crushed and desperate air our hero looked about him.

"It's . . . it's Krestyan Ivanovitch Rutenspitz, doctor of medicine and surgery; your old acquaintance, Yakov Petrovitch!" a detestable voice whispered in Mr. Golyadkin's ear. He looked round: it was Mr. Golyadkin's twin, so revolting in the despicable meanness of his soul. A malicious, indecent joy shone in his countenance; he was rubbing his hands with rapture, he was turning his head from side to side in ecstasy, he was fawning round every one in delight and seemed ready to dance with glee. At last he pranced forward, took a candle from one of the servants and walked in front, showing the way to Mr. Golyadkin and Krestyan Ivanovitch. Mr. Golyadkin heard the whole party in the drawing-room rush out after him, crowding and squeezing one another, and all beginning to repeat after Mr. Golyadkin himself, "It is all right, don't be afraid, Yakov Petrovitch; this is your old friend and acquaintance, you know, Krestyan Ivanovitch Rutenspitz. . . ."

At last they came out on the brightly lighted stairs; there was a crowd of people on the stairs too. The front door was thrown open noisily, and Mr. Golyadkin found himself on the steps, together with Krestyan Ivanovitch. At the entrance stood a carriage with four horses that were snorting with impatience. The malignant Mr. Golyadkin junior in three bounds flew down the stairs and opened the carriage door himself. Krestyan Ivanovitch, with an impressive gesture, asked Mr. Golyadkin to get in. There was no need of the impressive gesture, however; there were plenty of people to help him in. . . . Faint with horror, Mr. Golyadkin looked back. The whole of the brightly lighted staircase was crowded with people; inquisitive eyes were looking at him from all sides; Olsufy Ivanovitch himself was sitting in his easy chair on the top landing, and watching all that took place with deep interest. Every one was waiting. A murmur of impatience passed through the crowd when Mr. Golyadkin looked back.

"I hope I have done nothing . . . nothing reprehensible . . . or that can call for severity . . . and general attention in regard to my official relations," our hero brought out in desperation. A clamour of talk rose all round him, all were shaking their heads, tears started from Mr. Golyadkin's eyes.

"In that case I'm ready. . . . I have full confidence . . . and I entrust my fate to Krestyan Ivanovitch. . . ."

No sooner had Mr. Golyadkin declared that he entrusted his fate to Krestyan Ivanovitch than a dreadful, deafening shout of joy came from all surrounding him and was repeated in a sinister echo through the whole of the waiting crowd. Then Krestyan Ivanovitch on one side and Andrey Filippovitch on the other helped Mr. Golyadkin into the carriage; his double, in his usual nasty way, was helping to get him in from behind. The unhappy Mr. Golyadkin senior took his last look on all and everything, and, shivering like a kitten that has been drenched with cold water—if the comparison may be permitted—got into the carriage. Krestyan Ivanovitch followed him in immediately. The carriage door slammed. There was a swish of the whip on the horses' backs . . . the horses started off. . . . The crowd dashed after Mr. Golyadkin. The shrill, furious shouts of his enemies pursued him by way of good wishes for his journey. For some time several persons were still running by the carriage that bore away Mr. Golyadkin; but by degrees they were left behind, till at last they had all disappeared. Mr. Golyadkin's unworthy twin kept up longer than any one. With his hands in the trouser pockets of his green uniform he ran on with a satisfied air, skipping first to one and then to the other side of the carriage, sometimes catching hold of the window-frame and hanging on by it, poking his head in at the window, and throwing farewell kisses to Mr. Golyadkin. But he began to get tired, he was less and less often to be seen, and at last vanished altogether. There was a dull ache in Mr. Golyadkin's heart; a hot rush of blood set Mr. Golyadkin's head throbbing; he felt stifled, he longed to unbutton himself—to bare his breast, to cover it with snow and pour cold water on it. He sank at last into forgetfulness. . . .

When he came to himself, he saw that the horses were taking him along an unfamiliar road. There were dark patches of copse on each side of it; it was desolate and deserted. Suddenly he almost swooned; two fiery eyes were staring at him in the darkness, and those two eyes were glittering with malignant, hellish glee. "That's not Krestyan

Ivanovitch! Who is it? Or is it he? It is. It is Krestyan Ivanovitch, but not the old Krestyan Ivanovitch, it's another Krestyan Ivanovitch! It's a terrible Krestyan Ivanovitch! . . ."

"Krestyan Ivanovitch, I . . . I believe . . . I'm all right, Krestyan Ivanovitch," our hero was beginning timidly in a trembling voice, hoping by his meekness and submission to soften the terrible Krestyan Ivanovitch a little.

"You get free quarters, wood, with light, and service, the which you deserve not," Krestyan Ivanovitch's answer rang out, stern and terrible as a judge's sentence.

Our hero shrieked and clutched his head in his hands. Alas! For a long while he had been haunted by a presentiment of this.